Sanctuary

Her First Knight, Volume 5

Ash Gray

Published by Ash Gray, 2022.

SANCTUARY

First edition. November 4, 2022.

ISBN: 979-8224206056

Written by Ash Gray.

Chapter 1

Soon after the Dragon of Almara had fallen prey to her own foolishness, the blizzard lifted completely, and clear blue skies spread their warmth over the snowbanks. A rainbow even appeared, shimmering innocently above, so that Ava pointed at it and giggled girlishly.

Walking beside Ethne, Lysa smiled gratefully at the rainbow in the sunny sky, reflecting that it would be spring soon and farmers would begin a new crop. The markets would be bursting, and cattle would be roaming the fields. Spring was her favorite time of year.

As they traveled down the road back toward Hastow, Lysa was still in shock that Ava was so willing to give up her own child just to retake her throne. In all the years she had known Ava, the princess had never cared about politics or ruling. It was as if entering the tomb of Queen Saraid had changed something in Ava forever, and now, there was no going back for her: she must become queen of Illa.

Liadan likewise seemed to have become determined to set Ava on the throne and was overwhelmed with the realization that she would rule the seven realms at Ava's side. The two of them could be seen sitting together at the campfire, cooing over the dragon egg – almost as if it were more their child than the actual babe growing in Ava's womb!

And that was another thing: it had been three days since Godga's cabin, and Ava was growing steadily rounder. Ethne had told Lysa that Wildoras pregnancies only took three weeks. Before long, Ava and Liadan would be parents!

It was all happening so fast. It was overwhelming to Lysa, and she was only a side observer, yet Ava and Liadan, who were directly involved, were so calm and matter-of-fact about it all.

"This is madness!" Lysa hissed at Ethne one evening when they were breaking camp.

Liadan and Ava were standing together over the fire as they warmed themselves a last time, smiling and exchanging happy whispers. Ava was still carrying the dragon egg in her makeshift sling and held it now over the flames. Lysa gasped: the silhouette of a baby dragon could be seen inside!

"What is madness?" said Ethne dismissively. "That our friends are happy? Oh, yes. Right madness that is."

Lysa glared over her shoulder at the Knight of the Sparrow. Ethne was squatting over her saddlebags and was rummaging through them as she packed them. Lysa drew near and stood over her impatiently.

"I knew you'd take her side," Lysa complained. "You don't care about anything so long as Liadan is happy."

"Yes. I'm a terrible friend," Ethne sarcastically agreed, not looking up.

Lysa scowled. "Ethne! Don't you think this is all happening too fast?"

Ethne paused and finally looked up. She was concerned now, having heard the terror in Lysa's voice. "I thought you were happy about going on a quest?" she said, confused.

"I was," Lysa admitted. "But that was before Ava said she was coming as well! Ethne, she's in no condition! Destroying the four watchtowers won't be some merry lark!" She took a halting step closer. "You *must* convince Liadan. Tell her to tell Ava to hold off this quest! At least until the babe is grown! We should away to a temple, where she may raise the child in secret. And when the child and the dragon are old enough to fend for themselves, only then should the campaign begin—"

"I have heard your counsel, fair Lysa," said Ava, startling Lysa to silence.

Lysa turned: Ava and Liadan were still standing over the fire, side by side. Ava was cradling the green dragon egg in her arms, and after being warmed over the fire, it was glittering more brightly than ever before. The brilliant color matched her eyes almost completely.

"And I shall heed it," Ava said, smiling.

Lysa hesitated. "You shall?"

"Yes," sighed Ava, who suddenly looked very tired. "I know I've been . . .hasty. It's just, it feels as if all the pieces are finally falling into place!" Her eyes glowed with excitement. "I feel like my destiny is calling me!" She glanced dotingly at Liadan (who smiled) and added, "*Our* destiny."

Liadan gazed down into Ava's doting eyes with soft affection.

Ava gazed dreamily at Liadan a moment before looking at Lysa again. "I finally understand my place in the world, and I only wish to seize it!"

Lysa shook her head. "And you *will*, princess! But not overnight!"

"As I said, I have heard your counsel, dear Lysa," Ava answered. "We shall place the quest aside, and we shall find a temple where I may give birth." She looked down at the egg in her arms. "To both my children."

Lysa paused. "Wait a minute. . . When the Godga asked for your second child. . . She meant the dragon, didn't she?"

Ava nodded unhappily. "The dragon shall help me drive out Endoreth and then . . ." She looked down at the egg sadly, and Liadan placed a comforting hand on her shoulder.

"I suppose that's better than surrendering your own child," said Lysa, relieved. She noticed tears behind Ava's eyes and was startled and confused by them: Ava was behaving as if the dragon were her actual child!

"Yes," Ava said hoarsely, though her agreement was so obviously a lie.

They broke camp and continued on foot to Hastow. Liadan and Ethne walked side by side at the head of the procession. Ethne was still carrying her saddle bags over her shoulder, and the bags jingled with the gold they had taken from Queen Saraid's tomb. Liadan walked calmly beside her, and the two knights were speaking in low voices. Lysa thought their whispered conversation seemed suspicious, for they kept glancing back at Ava and looking quickly away. What were they up to?

"Lysa, I wish to ask something of you," said Ava. She was walking beside Lysa and had been in deep contemplation for some time, gazing off at the trees ahead, her pale lashes fluttering. Now she pushed the hair behind her ear as she said, "When I am queen, I shall need an advisor." Ava waited.

Lysa hesitated, caught completely off-guard. "And you would ask me?" she said in wonder. She had to admit she was flattered.

"I know you wanted to travel and go questing," Ava said quickly, "and you could still do that! But your advice has proven quite valuable to me, and I trust you. I l-love you," she said, blushing brightly.

Lysa felt her heart flutter, and inside her leather trousers, her sex was throbbing.

"And I couldn't imagine anyone more fit to help me rule. You would forever be a part of my court—"

Lysa halted and took Ava's hands. They faced each other, and Ava blushed hotter as Lysa said, "Nothing could honor me more greatly, my princess. I love you too." So saying, Lysa bounced up on tiptoe and kissed Ava slowly on the lips.

Ava's lashes fluttered and she smiled, quite flustered and pleased.

They walked on, and now Lysa was distracted with thoughts of making sweet love to Ava. She had meditated on it often as a girl, caressing Ava's big breasts, tasting her pink sex and the soft golden hair between her thighs. And since the night Liadan had taken them, her desire had only grown twofold. Oh, what would it be like to have Ava to herself? And would Ethne care? Would it anger her? Ethne was so possessive. Lysa knew she would probably never hear the end of it. But why? It wasn't as if she and Ethne were married!

Ethne had asked days before, and Lysa still hadn't given her answer. At the time, she had assumed Ethne was joking or delirious from her battle wounds, but now Lysa was realizing exactly how serious Ethne was about marriage. The woman kept sending her longing looks, sometimes tinged with sadness. It made Lysa feel terrible.

But Lysa didn't want to marry Ethne, and she didn't want to live in Ava's court as a royal counselor! She wanted to sail a ship on the open sea, make love to many fine women, and steal gold and jewels from the rich and greedy! Since her horrible stay in Bella's room, she had not been able to get the woman's riches out of her mind. There had been so much gold and jewelry and fine things, and Bella hadn't slogged away scrubbing chamber pots to get it, either.

No. No one became rich by slaving for the rich! No one deserved to be a chambermaid! Bella had taken what the world owed her! And while Bella had been a violent monster, Lysa couldn't help admiring the carefree and lavish aspects of the pirate lifestyle. She had already decided that, once this business with Endoreth was over, she was going to join a pirate crew and live life on the sea, above and beyond the reach of the law.

They walked all night, until finally, the gray dawn crept over the horizon, reaching its long fingers between the trees. Lysa was exhausted and just thinking how wonderful it would be to make camp and lie down when Liadan said with a sigh of relief, "At last – Hastow!"

Chapter 2

Hastow was indeed just ahead. They rounded the bend in the road, and there it was, a sea of fat little cruck houses and their thatched rooftops, chugging smoke from warm hearths as they spread away to the misty horizon and the sun that rose pale above the spidery treetops. Snow capped every roof and every naked tree, and sheets of ice spread over the road, so that men and women alike were out in the dawn, spreading sand to free the pavement.

On the hill, looming above the little town, was the temple of Eyslath, a beautiful stone building, ancient as it was large, with battlements from its days as a fortress and the red banners of the love goddess lifting in the wind from its towers. The center-most road in Hastow led right to it, though Ethne suggested that they get cleaned up and fed at a tavern first, so as not to be a burden on the sisters at the temple. Ava agreed, and so they found themselves renting a room at the Goddess Pearl, an inn so named because it was believed it had been blessed by the local goddess herself and was beloved of her.

"I will head downstairs and send a raven to my sister," Liadan said when they were in their room. She was standing by the hearth and lit a fire on it with a gentle gesture of her hand. A gold fireball the size of a melon floomed from her spread fingers and onto the logs, where it blazed gently.

"It will give Saoirse and Rowan time to get the ceremony underway," Liadan added, removing her gauntlets and warming her hands over the blaze. "And I imagine they'll want to start preparing the feast as well."

"Go then," agreed Ethne. "I will stay and mind the maidens." She and Liadan exchanged glances, making Ava go still.

Ava had been standing at the window, peering dreamily at the temple on the distant hill, but now she stared suspiciously at Liadan and Ethne, who were both avoiding her eye.

Lysa, however, didn't notice the silent exchange between the knights. Her back was to them as she unbuckled her scabbard and let her sword slide off. She scowled at Ethne's words. "I am not a maiden to be minded!" she declared. "I could protect Ava just as well!"

Ethne, for some bizarre reason, didn't bother arguing, instead removing her gauntlets. She sat in a corner chair and set about unbuckling the rest of her armor, and Lysa – though still looking cross – moved across the room to help her.

Liadan came to Ava and kissed her on the cheek in farewell. When she pulled back, Ava thought the Knight of the Wild had an odd sort of satisfied smile. She was half-tempted to grab Liadan and demand to know what was happening, but the knight moved away and was gone too quickly, as if to avoid any questions.

Suddenly feeling very sleepy and tired, Ava gave up trying to figure it out and yawned as she untied her fur cloak. The room had a large bathing basin near the hearth, and she could have sent for water, but she was just too tired to conceive of a bath at the moment. Perhaps later, after her nap.

Ava carefully unslung the dragon egg from around her neck and shoulders and set it on the corner table near Ethne, allowing it to sit in the nest of fabric there. She had been sleeping with it in her arms for days, its warmth pulsing against her body as the tiny dragon squirmed inside, but now she felt safe enough to set it aside. It was just close enough to the hearth that she knew the fire's warmth would help it along. Soon enough, it would hatch, and then she would have a baby dragon! The excitement tingled through her every day. A baby dragon, so cute and small, and one day, it would be mighty and fierce, and she would ride it into battle and drive out Endoreth and foul King Bjorn! They would paint the battle in murals on the walls of her tomb, and all would remember her as Ava the Liberator of Women, the Queen of Queens—

"What *are* you doing?" said Lysa, her amused voice shattering Ava's thoughts. "You do nothing these days but stare and stare at that blasted egg."

"Are you jealous, Lysa? Are you wishing the princess would pay you mind?" teased Ethne.

"No!" Lysa protested at once, and Ethne laughed, though Ava thought the knight's laughter a little . . . sad. Had Ethne seen them kiss on the road?

Ava felt guilty for allowing the kiss to happen. She was slowly beginning to notice that Ethne knew about Lysa's feelings for her. Perhaps Ethne had always known.

Ava glanced over her shoulder and was startled to realize Ethne had moved away from the table and was sitting on the edge of the bed in nothing but her underarmor. Her dark brown hair was loose of its usually low bun and was down around her shoulders. Ava had never seen it down before and was surprised by how long and beautiful it was. Sometimes she forgot how attractive Ethne was, with her slanted gray eyes and smirking lips. And now that she was in nothing but her underarmor, the bulging of the knight's strong arms and legs were apparent. She was sitting with her legs spread, leaning forward, elbows on her knees, and was watching Ava intently with great amusement.

Lysa, meanwhile, had taken Ava's place at the window. She was standing with her arms folded as she gazed out, and instead of removing her leather armor, it was still buckled on her body. Her sword, however, had been set across the seat of a nearby chair and was still in its leather sheath.

"I shall take first watch," Lysa said, gazing out the window. "You two take your rest. We only have two hours, then we head for the temple. We should not linger here long."

Ethne frowned, though her lips were twisted in a very amused smile. "So *commanding*, my lady," she teased Lysa. "What is your fear? The Dragon of Almara is slain – by your trap, no less – and the king of Illa has no interest in pursuing us. There is no need to be so grimly on-guard."

Lysa laughed flatly and did not relax her purposeful stance at the window. "Says you. Liadan still has a bounty on her head, lest you forget! And so do you, remember? We are not safe until we are in that temple and can claim sanctuary!"

"As you wish, my lady," said Ethne. She caught Ava's eye and winked. "Come," she said, patting the bed beside her. "I will help you out of that gown."

Ava looked into Ethne's eyes and saw the flame of lust there. Her heart skipped a beat, and caught somewhere between flattery and surprise, she moved toward the bed and sat on it beside Ethne. To her further surprise, Ethne slid her hard, strong legs around Ava, enclosing her from behind. Ava's heart beat faster in her chest. But surely, Ethne was not seducing her! She had never had any reason to believe Ethne wanted her.

Ethne started unlacing the back of Ava's gown and then – making Ava's heart pound in her chest – the Knight of the Sparrow carefully smoothed aside Ava's long golden hair and kissed the bare flesh of her neck and shoulder. They were slow, careful kisses that left Ava shivering in their wake. She was ashamed of herself when her sex responded, pulsing immediately with hunger. She could already feel the fat lips swelling between her thighs and squeezed them together, admonishing herself.

"Ethne!" Ava whispered, astonished yet breathless as Ethne's careful kisses continued. "W-What are you—?"

"Liadan told me to distract you and keep you in this room," Ethne answered between kisses. She paused, fumbling almost irritably with the laces on the back of Ava's blue traveling gown again. "Even if that meant fucking you – Blast these laces!"

Ava blushed to her hairline. "What?! Why?"

"It's a surprise," Ethne answered absently, for she had managed at last to get the laces loose, and Ava's gown tumbled down around her lap, revealing her large, naked breasts and how they stood plump and supple above her narrow waist. Her pink nipples were already hard with desire, and she hated herself for it. She took a shaking breath, causing her great breasts to lift with it, and she heard Ethne moan with longing behind her.

"Holy shite, your tits are perfect," Ethne whispered, her breath tickling Ava's ear. She smoothed her hands under, testing the heft of Ava's great breasts, then she slowly began to massage, rolling Ava's soft breasts in her strong hands and thumbing the nipples until they hardened further. Ava bit her lip to keep from moaning as the pleasure made her clit pulse.

"I'm almost jealous of Liadan," Ethne said quietly. "She gets to suck on these the rest of her life." She kissed Ava's shoulder again and squeezed both breasts with longing.

"Ethne!" Ava cried, astonished and trembling. "Such filthy talk!"

Ethne only chuckled. "Do you want me to stop?" she whispered.

"N-No," Ava admitted, blushing.

"As my lady commands," said Ethne playfully. She continued gently massaging Ava's breasts. One hand slid down to Ava's lap, where she pushed the mound of fallen fabric aside to reveal Ava's linen panties. Ava's thighs were tight together, and Ethne slid her hand between, relishing in how soft and warm they were, before prying them apart. Her hand slid down the front of Ava's panties and caressed gently at her pulsing clitoris, nudging it to hotter, harder pulsing, so that Ava sighed and frowned, letting her head fall back against Ethne in a daze of pleasure. She thought she would melt into the knight and disappear.

When Ava glanced up, Ethne was looking down at her with soft gray eyes. She kissed Ava without warning on the lips – and with such sweet passion that Ava felt herself melting again. They kissed for a long moment, as Ethne gently groped and fingered, and when their lips pulled apart, Ethne buried another kiss in Ava's shoulder and squeezed both of her breasts again, hard, so that her cleavage rose in swelling mounds. Ava gasped with delight.

"I have a strap," Ethne whispered in Ava's ear, tugging her panties down around her hips, until they tumbled around her ankles. "I've never used it on Lysa."

Ava didn't know what a strap was, and her green eyes grew round. But at the mention of Lysa, she looked over to the window, blushing with embarrassment and suddenly wondering why the handmaiden had not protested, intervened, *something*. It was so unlike Lysa to have remained quiet!

When Ava looked over, she was surprised to see Lysa simply standing there. The handmaiden's arms were no longer folded and were hanging lifeless at her sides. She was facing away from the window and was staring at them, completely frozen. Her mouth was hanging open and her eyes were glazed with lust. She was staring directly at Ava, staring with such a hunger that Ava felt her sex thump. She had never seen Lysa look at her that way before!

"Lysa," Ethne called with a laugh, "has your soul flown from your body?"

Lysa didn't answer, instead turning beet red and glaring at Ethne.

Ethne smiled. "Well? You want Ava, do you not? You think of her night and day. It's why you won't marry me, isn't it? Because you love her! You love Ava!"

Lysa swallowed hard and didn't answer.

"Well, here she is," said Ethne scathingly, and Ava gasped when Ethne grabbed her thighs and roughly spread her legs, snapping them apart to reveal her pink sex and the curly golden hair there.

To Ava's surprise, Lysa stared at her sex with soft-eyed longing. She licked her lips, but she didn't move. "Stop this, Ethne!" she cried at last.

"Yes, Ethne, don't do this to her!" Ava scolded.

"Do what?" said Ethne darkly. "Reveal the truth of things? Lysa watched as I played you like a lute, and she enjoyed it because she wants to fuck you herself." So saying, Ethne slid two fingers in Ava's moist sex and caressed her deeply, while her other hand cupped and massaged one of Ava's heavy breasts.

Ava couldn't help herself: as Lysa watched, she wiggled and moaned in Ethne's grasp, and the moisture of her sex began sliding down her thighs, which were trembling from the strain of holding back.

"Oh *goddess*," Ava whispered, pink-cheeked and staring at the ceiling as her belly tightened against the threat of a climax. Ethne's fingers were so deliciously careful and skilled. She really was playing Ava like a lute, and she liked it. Gods help her, she liked it!

"Come, Lysa," Ethne said darkly. "You can't resist her. You want her!"

Lysa was trembling all over and her brown eyes were suffering. As if something had broken in her chest, she dashed across the room and fell to her knees between Ava's thighs, and to Ava's astonishment, she buried her face in Ava's sex and ate her out as ravenous as a hog at a trough.

Ava's helpless screams filled the room as she climaxed.

LATER WHEN AVA WAS sleeping in the large bed, Lysa rose naked from the bed and went to the washbasin on the bedside table and splashed her face clean. She knew now that the kiss on the road had been a mistake—for it was clear now that Ethne had seen – and she felt ashamed of herself for giving in to her lust. She had always wanted to maintain a strict friendship between herself and Ava. She had never wanted Ava to figure out just how badly she wanted her, for she did not want Ava's pity and discomfort to sully their friendship. Even when they had made love with Liadan, Lysa had shown restraint, allowing Ava to dominate her in their kissing and not the other way around. Now Lysa's feelings had been made plain, and she felt naked, exposed, vulnerable. Ava knew about her. Ava knew.

Looking very smug, Ethne came near Lysa and sat on the edge of the bed. She was still wearing her underarmor, which looked like long underwear, and her long brown hair was tousled from having lain on her back while Ava sat on her face . . . as Lysa rode Ethne's strap . . . as she and Lysa kissed on top of Ethne.

Lysa had never been penetrated before. Ethne's strap was a phallic sex toy made of soft sheepskin. Lysa had buckled it on her, heart beating with anticipation, and then had slowly sat on it. She would never forget how it felt when the phallus slowly filled her sex that first time, plunging deep inside and stroking her so deliciously. And Ethne, so big and strong, had taken Lysa by the hips and moved her gently up and down on it, until she was riding the strap in slow rhythm, her head falling back in a gasp of baffled ecstasy.

Ava had watched for a while as Lysa rode Ethne's strap, blushing all the while, her green eyes bright with lust, before Ethne had easily lifted the princess up and then down on her face. And so it was that Lysa and Ava had kissed hungrily as they rode Ethne, who lay beneath them, enjoying herself immensely.

But as much as Lysa had enjoyed herself, she could not even look at Ethne now. She was furious. Ethne was still wearing the strap, and it stood erect from her hips, still glossy with the moisture of Lysa's sex. Lysa blushed with shame to see just how wet the strap was. And because of Ava. Because of Lysa's lust for Ava! Ethne knew it too, and there was something bitter about her smile when she looked at Lysa.

"Why didn't you just tell me you loved Ava?" Ethne said quietly, so as not to wake the princess, who slept peacefully on the bed behind her. "Then I wouldn't have made a fool of myself these past few weeks, professing my love and carrying on. You care nothing for me. This was all about sex, wasn't it?"

Lysa had been dabbing her face with a kerchief, but she paused and said at once, "That is not true!"

Ethne didn't seem convinced. She pulled her own kerchief from inside the collar of her underarmor – Lysa noticed with a miserable blush that it was the green favor she had given Ethne weeks before – then dipped it in the washbasin and started polishing the strap clean. Her gray eyes laughed when Lysa blushed a little.

"I was going to fuck you with it on our wedding night," Ethne said, looking down at the strap as she cleaned it. "I was going to surprise you. I guess it doesn't matter now. You'll go off and be a bandit queen or whatever the hell, and I'll . . ." She sighed. "I guess I'll stay with Liadan and help her in this mad quest to become queen of the world." She laughed tonelessly. "At least Liadan still needs me."

"Oh, Ethne," Lysa said soothingly, overcome with misery and compassion. She reached over and touched Ethne's cheek, so that the Knight of the Sparrow stopped polishing the strap and looked up at her.

"You're my first knight!" Lysa said in exasperation and smiled. "Of *course*, I care about you! And nothing shall ever change that!"

Lysa was glad when Ethne seemed pleased, but the Knight of the Sparrow gave a sad half-smile as she said, "Of course, you care about me. You just don't *love* me. And I need that. I need you to love me."

"Oh, Ethne," Lysa said miserably again. Ethne was speaking as if Lysa could just force herself to love her instead of Ava. Hearts didn't work that way.

With heavy, sad movements, Ethne reached over and drew Lysa near, hugging the smaller woman between her thighs. Lysa slid her arms around Ethne's neck and gazed down at her, thinking that she was so strong and so beautiful. It was rare that Ethne, being so tall, was ever in a position beneath Lysa, but the knight was sitting on the low bed. Lysa's perky little breasts were near Ethne's face, and she looked down at them, eyes glazed with lust.

Without warning, Ethne kissed Lysa tenderly on the mouth. As ever, her kisses were soft and slow, yet hungry, her tongue occasionally thrusting against Lysa's. Lysa's heart was fluttering with delight, and as they kissed, Ethne smoothed her hands over Lysa's soft backside and lifted her up . . . and then down on the strap.

Lysa gasped as the sheepskin phallus slowly plunged between the tight lips of her sex, filling her to the base as Ethne gently pulled her hips down. Her eyes widened as she was filled, then hooded as the pleasure throbbed in her sex. Lysa moaned and tightened her arms around Ethne's neck, and when she looked down, the knight was gazing up at her with such soft longing, she felt an ache in her chest. What had she done to deserve Ethne's love? Why her? Ethne had never loved before. All the women in her past had been playthings, yet she was fixated on Lysa.

Gazing with intent hunger into Lysa's eyes, Ethne guided the handmaiden's hips, until Lysa was riding the strap on her own, her shapely little body moving fluidly against Ethne, who enjoyed the crush of her soft flesh. Ethne, eyes soft, kissed Lysa's lips gently, again and again, pausing to gaze at her with the same doting look that made Lysa suddenly weep.

Ethne paused. "Why are you crying?" she whispered. "Is it the strap, does it hurt—?"

"No, no," said Lysa, shaking her head. She tightened her thighs to stop Ethne from lifting her off. When Ethne hugged her waist again, she started slowly riding and moaned as the phallus filled her. But the tears kept coming. Her head fell back with another sigh of pleasure, and her skin tingled when Ethne kissed her neck and cleavage.

"Then why do you weep, sweet Lysa?" Ethne whispered. "Are they happy tears?"

Their lips found each other again and they kissed. They peered into each other's eyes, their noses brushing as Lysa continued to ride, and Lysa confessed in a miserable whisper, "I have never been so loved! Yet I cannot love you in return. I fear I shall break thee!"

Ethne smiled and seemed very pleased by the confession. "You wound me, tis true. But it will heal, sweet Lysa." She kissed Lysa's lips and whispered against them, "Hush now, and make love to me."

Lysa smiled at the playful command, and gyrated her hips slowly, letting her soft body crush against Ethne. She smoothed her small hand through the back of Ethne's hair, thinking the Knight of the Sparrow so beautiful, and as they kissed again, her sex tightened on strap, and she climaxed.

Chapter 3

When Liadan returned from the smithy with her purchase tucked away in her cloak, it was afternoon, and the tavern below the inn was now full of patrons, music, and noise. She glanced over the many-colored heads of the crowd and did not spot Ava, Lysa, or Ethne in their midst, but she was pleasantly surprised to spot the familiar red head of her sister, Ceana, who was seated at the bar and enjoying a pint.

Ceana was Liadan's older sister, but she possessed such a sweet, youthful face that she might as well have been Liadan's younger sister. Unlike Liadan, her red hair was straighter and much more tamed, falling down the silver back of her beautifully engraved armor in a red river of tresses. She sensed Liadan before she saw her, so strong were her magi senses, and her head turned the moment Liadan stepped through the tavern door. Their eyes connected, and Ceana smiled, as if she had been waiting for Liadan to notice her.

Ceana waved Liadan over, and Liadan gave the rare grin, pushing her way through the crowds and to the bar. When they met, they hugged, slapping each other hard on the back. Then Ceana retook her seat on a barstool and took up her pint again.

"Knights of the temple are not allowed to drink," Liadan said, taking a seat beside her sister at the bar.

Ceana only rolled her eyes, smiled, and tipped back her mug of ale. On her back was a giant two-handed blade, a beautifully crafted silver sword identical to the ones all knights carried who served in the temple.

17

Unlike Liadan, Ceana's face was fresh and clean of warpaint, and she was wearing a beautiful red cape to match the banners of the goddess Eyslath, who she was sworn to serve.

In truth, Liadan was not surprised that Ceana had ignored her vows and was drinking. Knights who served in temples were expected to remain pure. They were not allowed to set foot in places like taverns, let alone consume anything beyond wine. They weren't even allowed to have sex. But Ceana had always been rebellious and largely indifferent when it came to customs and traditions. Out of all of Liadan's sisters, she was the one who had adapted most readily to having been sent forth from Wildoras. Liadan and her other sisters were more traditional and reverent of the Old Gods.

"So you received my raven," Liadan said crossly. "Yet you thought it a good idea to come down here to a place you are forbidden to enter?" She gestured at the barkeep for a drink, and the crooked little man slid a tankard to her across the bar.

"I received your raven, little sister," Ceana confirmed, looking somewhere between amused and exasperated. "No doubt you are itching to scold me for coming here. I know I am not allowed."

"Yes, I confess it is tempting to scold you," Liadan admitted, frowning, "but I know you shall not listen. You were always set in your ways. I just don't want to see you punished for coming here to see me. You could have waited at the temple! What if they expel you?"

Ceana sighed, as if to say Liadan's lecturing was typical. "This time I came to guard one of the sisters," she said calmly. "I have permission to be here."

Liadan went still. Ceana looked back at her, amused.

"Then where is this sister?" Liadan demanded skeptically.

Ceana nodded.

Liadan followed her sister's gaze and saw a beautiful young woman standing on the other side of the tavern. She was wearing a long red robe that hid her figure entirely, but wisps of blonde hair peeped from her hood, which was drawn up over her head, and her small face was sweet and pretty. Around her narrow waist was a heavy chain-belt, and to the belt was tethered a book, the holy word of Eyslath. She was reading from the book to a crowd of drunken men and women, who were hooting and throwing peanuts at her. The woman, not to be deterred, kept reading, even as peanuts bounced off her face.

"She is Sister Fionn," said Ceana, who suddenly sounded very tired, "and when she learned you had come, she insisted on escorting me down here as an excuse to 'save souls.' If she catches me drinking, I'll never hear the end of it, so when she comes over here, just say my pint is yours."

Liadan shook her head in disapproval but said with a laugh, "Fine." She tipped back her own tankard for a gulp.

"What kept you in town, anyway?" Ceana asked. "I've been waiting a little more than an hour."

Liadan smiled, reached inside her fur cloak, and pulled out a small package. She slid it across the bar to Ceana, who pried the package open to reveal a small box. Her curiosity aroused, Ceana pushed aside her drink and opened the lid of the box. Inside was a beautiful golden ring with a green gem.

"Ah," said Ceana, "this is for the princess you did ruin your life for."

Liadan scowled. "I told Ava that you were sweet and that you would love her. You must be kind to her when you meet. She and the others should be down for the noon meal soon."

"As you wish," said Ceana, sliding the package back across the bar to Liadan. "But I cannot pretend I am pleased that you have gotten yourself caught up in that woman's chaos."

Liadan frowned. "I thought you would be happy for me."

"Aye," said Ceana. "You are a romantic sort, and you aren't fit to be alone. I always wanted marriage and children for you. But with her? She's a Damaris. She was exiled from her home and all her trinkets and baubles were taken from her, all her pretty gowns and tiaras, her titles, her pretty slippers. A Damaris will never stand for that – not if they've a spine. And once Princess Ava goes on her crusade to take back Caradin, once she has her baubles and gowns back, do you think she's going to shack up with you? You're a barbarian, exiled from your homeland, forbidden to rule." Ceana waved dismissively. "She'll find a lover with a title and forget all about you."

Liadan's face darkened. "How can you say such vile things to me?! You don't even know Ava—!"

"But I know her house," said Ceana over Liadan. "You've only just left the academy, little sister. I've been traveling around Illa a lot longer than you have. I know the history here. I know what the royal house is like. They are not friends of Wildoras. Ava will use you and then she'll leave you, mark my words."

Liadan scowled. "Ava would never. Never!"

Ceana nodded, as if Liadan's protests were to be expected. "Yes, yes. Love is blind, and you're a sensitive romantic, gods help you. I knew you wouldn't listen to me. Here . . . I've got you a wedding present." So saying, Ceana reached inside her red cape and pulled out a narrow, long package. She slid it across the bar to Liadan, who caught it under her gauntlet and picked it up.

Liadan squeezed the package and eyed her sister suspiciously. "This feels like a banana," she said awkwardly.

Ceana chuckled. "Don't open it here," she said, taking a gulp from her pint. She licked her lips and set the pint down. "It's a strap."

Liadan blushed a little. "Th-Thank you," she muttered, putting the package away in her cloak.

Ceana chuckled again.

Just then, Sister Fionn strode over, chin lifted, looking rather grave. "Knight Ceana! Are you *drinking*?"

"Of course not, sister," said Ceana at once, pushing her tankard away.

Liadan held back a laugh.

Fionn's eyes turned to the Knight of the Wild. "And this must be your sister. Hello, Liadan," she said, very prim and proper. "I am Sister Fionn." She bowed, folding her hands in prayer before her.

"Well met, sister," Liadan returned. "Have you come here to drink?" she teased.

Ceana held back a smile as Sister Fionn's cheeks flushed pink.

"D-Drink!" cried the sister, appalled. "You *must* be jesting."

"So you've come to have your honeypot licked then," Liadan went on, completely straight-faced, and Fionn blushed right to her hairline.

"H-Ha!" cried the sister nervously, her face now scarlet. "You are rather like Ceana after all. She is always taunting." She glanced at Ceana fondly, and she was standing so close now that Liadan could see her pretty, slanted eyes were the palest blue. She was quite fair all around. Liadan wondered what was under her robe.

"Shall we stay and partake the noon meal with your sister's party?" Fionn asked Ceana. She glanced away across the room. "I do see a few souls that may be salvageable, though most seem drunk beyond all hope."

"We can stay, why not?" agreed Ceana.

Sister Fionn seemed pleased by that. She smiled serenely and turned away, moving once again into the crowds with her holy book. People threw peanuts and almonds at her as she passed, but she kept reading scriptures with a sort of grim determination.

"Are you fucking her?" Liadan asked when Fionn was out of earshot.

Ceana snorted, taking her pint in hand again. "I wish," she said, tipping the pint back for a gulp. "Serving in the temple is the purest, most peaceful hell, day and night."

Liadan looked around at her sister in amusement. "What do you mean?"

Ceana set her pint down, staring bitterly at Sister Fionn, who was now across the room being pelted with stale bread. "I have seen all of the sisters naked – all one hundred and fifty-two of them. They require an escort everywhere they go to ensure they never break their vows and lay with a man. And so, I must watch them bathe, change robes . . . go down on each other."

Liadan laughed in amazement. "You jest!"

"Again—I wish," said Ceana wearily. "They are not allowed to lay with men or their knights or anyone outside the temple, but they *are* allowed to lay with other sisters. And I, restricted from touching them as I am, must watch as they make love ceaselessly." She shook her head again and took another bitter gulp from her pint. It was now empty. She waved at the barkeep for another.

"I don't know why you haven't cracked," said Liadan with great sympathy. "And to think Ethne and I were going to take vows and become temple guardians at your side."

Ceana laughed dryly. "Ethne wouldn't have lasted one day without pussy."

Liadan laughed as well. "True enough." She jerked her head at the sister. "So is Fionn a virgin? How sweet and innocent is she really?"

Ceana laughed, catching her new pint when the barkeep slid it to her. "What you see is exactly what you receive: Fionn is as sweet and virginal as she doth appear. Many in the temple have tried to lay with her, including Mother Tiede, who's a hungry old dragon, if I dare say so, and quite in love with Fionn. Fionn has turned away all. She insists she is given already to the goddess and that she mustn't anger Eyslath by lying with another."

Liadan frowned. "Really? Eyslath is a goddess of love. She would *want* her followers to have sex, wouldn't she?"

Ceana shrugged. "I suspect young Fionn is still burdened by her past."

"What do you mean?" Liadan asked with dread.

"Her village was burned when she was a girl," said Ceana heavily. "She witnessed many horrors, saw women raped and bloodied in the streets. She doesn't even understand what sex is. She thinks it's rape."

"Ah. So she is afraid to let others touch her," said Liadan, nodding and tossing back her pint for a gulp.

"Aye," said Ceana in a low voice. "And you had best warn your hound of a friend to leave Fionn be. She shall regret it otherwise." So saying, she nodded at the stairs.

Liadan followed Ceana's gaze and saw Ethne coming down the stairs with Ava and Lysa. Ava looked radiant, her little tummy protruding with the first signs of pregnancy. She grinned when she saw Liadan and hurried faster down the stairs, lifting her skirts in both hands. Several heads turned in a ripple as Ava came rushing down, men and women alike admiring her beauty.

Let them look, let them drool, Liadan thought proudly. *She is the greatest beauty in Illa, and she is mine!*

"Be careful, princess!" Lysa begged, taking Ava's arm. "The child!"

But Ava was determined to get to Liadan and ignored Lysa's fussing, descending the stairs at the same reckless pace.

"Gods be *good,*" growled Ceana, leaning forward and speaking low. She sounded furious. "Did you already get that little girl *pregnant*?"

"Yes," Liadan admitted wretchedly.

"She looks like a babe herself! I should take you out and pummel you for being so foolhardy," Ceana said in amazement.

Liadan frowned miserably. "I couldn't help it! I love her, Ceana. Do you understand that? I love her! And my body reacted, and now . . ."

"Yes, yes," apologized Ceana, rubbing Liadan's shoulder. "I know, I know."

"Be kind to her when she approaches," begged Liadan. "She has been through so much."

"*You* have been through so much!" Ceana hissed in a low voice. "You have given up everything—!"

"It was my choice—!"

"The hell it was! She took advantage of your soft heart. Or rather, your soft head—!"

Liadan glared. "Ceana—please!"

Ceana didn't have a chance to continue the argument, for Ava crushed into Liadan, hugging her tightly around the neck.

"You are back, my love!" Ava cried, hugging Liadan's neck and kissing her cheek again and again.

Liadan felt the joy bubbling in her to have Ava's soft, sweet body in her arms again. She pulled back, and they kissed happily. Then she easily pulled Ava onto her lap, and thus they sat at the bar together.

Ethne took a seat beside Liadan and tried to pull Lysa onto her lap in a similar manner, but Lysa smacked Ethne's hands off and climbed onto her own barstool. Crestfallen, Ethne waved at the barkeep and ordered herself the noon meal.

"The noon meal for all of us, actually," called Liadan to the barkeep and reached in her cloak, pulling out her coin purse. She pulled out the little package with the ring and set it on the bar before Ava.

Ava paused, her pale lashes fluttering prettily when she saw the package. "But . . ." She hesitated. "What is it?" she cried, looking up at Liadan with girlishly bright eyes.

Liadan hugged Ava and said in her ear, "Open it and see."

Small hands trembling a little with anticipation, Ava carefully pried the package open and lifted the lid of the little box. She screamed happily when she saw the ring and nearly dropped it, causing several heads to turn around the tavern. "Oh, Liadan!" she cried in ecstasy. "It's beautiful! Beautiful! Shall we wed at the temple? With Saoirse and Rowan?"

"If it pleases my love," Liadan answered, and Ava squealed with joy.

"A double wedding!" sighed Lysa happily.

"Double the drinks," joked Ethne, though Liadan thought she looked a little sad.

Liadan took the ring from the box and carefully slid it on Ava's slender finger. They kissed, then Liadan hugged Ava tight from behind, and Ava held out her hand, gleefully admiring the ring.

Ceana darkly cleared her throat.

"Ava," said Liadan, "allow me to introduce my sister, Knight Ceana of Hastow. Ceana, this is fair Princess Ava, soon to be queen of Illa and the seven realms . . . and the love of my life."

"You're twenty! You haven't lived!" dismissed Ceana, whose bitter words made Ava pause. Ceana politely inclined her head to the princess, her expression cold. "Well met, Princess Ava. I trust you are well?"

Ava opened her mouth to respond, but Ceana didn't give her a chance to, instead saying over her, "I should see if Sister Fionn is ready to depart. It isn't good for the sisters to linger in such places. Good day." And with that, she had gone.

Ava blinked after Ceana in astonishment, likely wondering what she had done to warrant such rudeness, and Liadan gazed after her sister as well and felt foolish for ever assuming overprotective Ceana would have approved of their match.

Chapter 4

The wedding was held at sunset, on the roof of the great temple, as dusk spread its watery, golden hues over the distant banks of snow surrounding Hastow. As a giant statue of six-armed Eyslath loomed above, Ava and Liadan, Rowan and Saoirse all stood together under the arch, each couple facing each other and holding hands, as Mother Tiede guided them through their vows. When the vows were spoken and each couple had kissed, the sisters tossed the petals of winter flowers high from their baskets, and the white petals spiraling slowly through the night air were like snowflakes as Liadan carried Ava beneath them.

The knights had removed their armor for the ceremony. Instead, they were wearing fine tunics and trousers, while Ava was wearing a beautiful white gown that Liadan had bought her and surprised her with just minutes before the ceremony, when she was fretting with Lysa about her torn traveling gown. Liadan had done a great deal of shopping while Ethne was keeping Ava . . . distracted.

Ethne had never seen Liadan so happy and glowing. She was truly happy for her friend and could not comprehend how Ceana would disapprove of her sister's love for Ava. During the ceremony, Ceana stood in the back in her green tunic and was the only one who looked sour, but when Mother Tiede asked if anyone was against the wedding, Liadan's sister did not speak out, instead remaining stony and silent at the back of the crowd.

Ethne had only met Ceana once before. It was during one of her year's quest tours around Illa, when she was still a girl at the academy. Ceana had taken a position at the temple to be nearer Liadan, and they had stopped at the temple during their tour, that Liadan might visit with her sister. Even back then, Ceana had been overprotective, lecturing Saoirse about looking out for her sister and keeping her safe, so that even calm, agreeable Saoirse was riled.

Ceana saw everyone and everything as a threat to Liadan, even Ethne, who she disliked greatly for constantly dragging Liadan into her messes.

Inside the temple, they drank, feasted, and danced the night away. To Ethne's astonishment, the sisters removed their heavy red robes, revealing the skimpy linen garments they wore beneath. These white linen garments were mere folds of cloth that fell over them front and back but left their sides completely exposed, so the sides of their breasts and buttocks were apparent. A single white rope was tied around their waists to keep the narrow linen in place, covering front and back, and so they went around, with flowers in their long hair, dancing half-naked with jiggling breasts and buttocks.

Ethne thought she would go mad, surrounded as she was by all the softness and sweetness she could not touch. Some of the sisters were older, wrinkled, and far past their prime, but most were young and beautiful and supple, their breasts high, their skin flawless. And Ethne wasn't allowed to touch any of them. Some of them teased her by shaking their breasts at her, and she thought she would snap, standing there with her clit throbbing behind her trousers.

The dancing went on all night, and it seemed everyone was paired up except for Ethne. She stood at the banquet table, tankard in hand, and watched as Liadan spun around the dance floor with Ava, watched as Saoirse and Rowan lifted little Lysa between them and kissed both her cheeks as they danced with her. Even Ceana and the temple knights were dancing with the sisters. But Ethne was alone.

Ethne gulped bitterly from her tankard and glared as Lysa was lifted onto big Rowan's hip like a child. Clutching little Lysa in one arm, Rowan put her other arm around Saoirse, and the two of them did a funny hop-kick dance together as Lysa clung to Rowan's neck and laughed. Breathless with laughter, Rowan looked at Lysa's lips and kissed her hungrily. Lysa was flustered and barely had time to catch her breath before Saoirse had kissed her next. The two big women were pressed close to her on either side, and because she was riding Rowan's hip, it was easy for them to reach her mouth. They closed in, kissing her lips and cheeks, as she sighed and blushed between them, closing her eyes and looking so soft and innocent . . .

But Lysa wasn't innocent at all, Ethne knew. She was a hungry little thing, always looking for pleasure, always aroused and lusting. Ethne looked at Lysa and wanted her, wanted to pry her away from Rowan and Saoirse, but she also didn't want to disrupt the party by starting a brawl, so she stood at the banquet table and seethed.

When some time had passed, Rowan and Saoirse decided to retire to their room for the night – and they took Lysa with them. When they turned from the room, Lysa was still riding Rowan's hip, cheeks flushed from wine and arousal. As they were leaving through the great wooden doors, Ethne saw Rowan's hand close on Lysa's backside and squeeze. Ethne felt a vein going in her temple. That was the last straw!

Not wanting to draw attention to herself, Ethne waited a beat, then set her tankard on the table and followed Rowan, Saoirse, and Lysa out into the torchlit corridor. Once there, it suddenly hit her that she hadn't a clue where Rowan and Saoirse's room was and that she would have to follow them at a distance, keeping very quiet and going unnoticed.

The three women were tipsy with wine, so it was easy enough for Ethne to follow them without being seen or heard. She hovered at the end of the hall and watched as they disappeared inside the bedroom.

Then very slowly, she approached the door, knelt at the keyhole, and listened.

Ethne's cheeks flamed furiously: there was already moaning and kissing happening inside! Very carefully, she closed her hand on the doorknob and turned, opening the door the slightest crack. What she saw inside froze her: Rowan was sitting on the edge of bed with Lysa in her lap, and she was hugging Lysa from behind as she carefully pushed up her tunic and undershirt, revealing her perky breasts. She cupped Lysa's small breasts in her strong hands, massaging them carefully, and Lysa was blushing as they kissed.

Saoirse, meanwhile, was kneeling before Lysa and carefully unbuckling her trousers. While Lysa was kissing Rowan and squirming in her grasp, Saoirse was inching Lysa's trousers and panties down. Lysa was being carefully stripped naked by both of them, and their hands were all over her. She was shivering between them as they kissed her skin and groped her breasts. Rowan found Lysa's lips again and kissed her hungrily on the mouth, and as Lysa was paralyzed by Rowan's groping and kissing, Saoirse was sucking on one of Lysa's breasts – suckling so hungrily that her face was buried in it. Her fingers slid in Lysa's sex as she suckled her, and Ethne watched, her clit pumping hard between her thighs, as Lysa's pink little sex sucked and clenched on Saoirse's fingers. The lips were already dripping.

Saoirse then leaned down between Lysa's legs and sucked on Lysa's clitoris as she fingered her, and Lysa melted, closed on both sides by the muscular women, helpless to their caressing and sucking and kissing. Damn Rowan and Saoirse! They had been after her woman since Hargendon! Ethne wanted to lunge into the room and beat them both to the floor, but her brain was clouded by wine and arousal, and all she could manage was to kneel there at the door and peep in, watching in bitterness and longing.

Tears in her eyes, Ethne staggered at last to her feet, turned, and marched fast down the corridor.

Chapter 5

Fionn felt a little light-headed. It wasn't often that she drank wine so heavily, for she was afraid the goddess Eyslath would frown upon it and perhaps punish her in some way. She felt ashamed for her sin and decided to head to the little shrine in the chapel and pray for forgiveness.

Slipping from the party, Fionn walked quickly up the hall and entered the chapel. Here, hundreds of candles were lit, glowing like a sea of stars in the otherwise dark room. There were little pillows on the wood-paneled floor for kneeling and praying, and at the far end of the aisle stood the shrine: a child-sized statue of six-armed Eyslath, who used her six arms to cradle a babe to her naked breasts. There were flowers and coins and other offerings at the foot of the shrine, incense was burning sweetly, and – to Fionn's surprise – there was a woman kneeling before the statue . . . kneeling and sobbing.

Fionn recognized the woman as one of the knights who had come to the temple for the wedding. She was a dark-haired beauty, her long hair falling in a neat plait down her back. When she had first come to the temple, she'd been wearing beautifully engraved silver armor, but now she wore an ornate tunic of a dark green material and tight brown trousers. She was on her knees on the pillow closest to the statue, her head was bowed, and she was holding something in her hand. Something . . . phallic.

"Are you all right?" Fionn asked sweetly, stepping awkwardly into the room. "Do you need help?"

The knight slowly looked around and froze, and Fionn knew what she must've looked like to her. Like the other sisters in the temple, Fionn had removed her red robes and was wearing her white linen under-robes for the festivities. This meant that only her front and back were covered, leaving her sides seductively exposed, and her yellow hair was long and loose around her shoulders, falling all the way to her backside. A flower tiara was also upon her head, made of white winter flowers, and her cheeks were flushed from her walk to the chapel.

Fionn blushed a little brighter as the knight gawped at her. The woman seemed to find her very attractive. Her eyes were bright with desire, but they were soft as well – not hard and cruel and foul as the men who had lusted after her, as Mother Tiede's eyes became when they were alone. No. This knight was gentle and good and saw her not just as desirable but as a person as well. Though knights usually terrified her, Fionn felt strangely unafraid. Smiling, she took another step into the room.

Embarrassed, the crying knight sniffed and looked away, wiping away her tears with the heel of her hand. "I'm f-fine," she lied. "I was just . . ."

"Were you praying to Eyslath?" asked Fionn, delighted. She drew near, and after hesitating, she knelt on a pillow beside the knight. Her round, innocent eyes fixed in childlike wonder on the statue, then she closed her eyes and smiled. The chapel had always given her so much peace, made her feel so safe – the chapel and the many armed knights.

"I was asking her to make someone love me," the knight confessed. She laughed dryly and more tears poured down her face. "I don't think she heard."

Fionn frowned sympathetically. "Who do you want to love you?"

The knight looked away. "It doesn't matter," she said bitterly. "I suppose it would be an evil thing to force someone to love me. Eyslath is right to ignore my selfish prayers. I suppose in my rage I did not reflect."

"You are most wise, fair knight," said Fionn, impressed. "Even in your rage."

The knight laughed again, looking around at Fionn fondly. She frowned. "Hey . . . You're that sister who was at the tavern earlier! The one who came with Ceana! I thought I recognized you . . . You're *beautiful*!" So saying, the knight reached out to touch Fionn's face.

Fionn shivered and nearly cringed away. After the things she had seen as Tuinhold burned, she never let anyone touch her. But for reasons she didn't understand, she wanted this knight to touch her. The knight seemed so helpless and drunk and harmless, and she was quite beautiful herself, with her pretty gray eyes and lips wet from wine. Fionn didn't feel afraid. And part of her was hungry, longing to be touched by someone . . . Someone beautiful and gentle like this sad, weeping knight.

But to Fionn's disappointment, the beautiful knight withdrew her hand and winced, saying apologetically, "I'm sorry. The wine has gone to my head. I shouldn't have tried to . . ." The knight fell silent and wobbled in place when Fionn put a finger against the woman's lips.

"It's all right," Fionn said with a girlish laugh, and her little thumb with its white, translucent nail smoothed away one of the knight's tears. The knight blushed at this. So cute, Fionn thought.

Fionn's eyes flitted down to the strange object in the woman's hand. It looked like a short rod, and it had buckles and straps hanging from it. Such an odd thing to carry about. Fionn's lashes fluttered. "But . . . what is that you carry, good knight?"

The knight gave a drunken half-smile, still wobbling in place. "It goes about the hips, like this, my lady . . ." So saying, she fumbled to buckle the contraption on, and when she was done, the rod was standing erect from her pelvis. Realizing at last what the object was, Fionn blushed to her hairline.

"Oh my!" Fionn cried.

"Don't be alarmed, sister!" the knight begged, holding out her hands. "I only had it with me because I was hoping . . . . I was hoping she would love me . . . And then we would make love . . ." The knight dropped her eyes and wept bitterly again, her strong shoulders shaking. She turned her back. "By the gods, don't watch me weep! I am pathetic for this . . . I shall die of shame."

"No, no," said Fionn soothingly. She hesitated and reached out, rubbing the knight's back. The firm muscles there startled her, and she felt her sex stir to pumping. She blushed prettily as arousal swept over her, but ignoring her feelings, she said kindly to the knight, "I think you are very sweet and gentle. I have never seen a knight cry before!"

"That does not make me feel better," said the knight with a toneless laugh, but she turned back around to face Fionn, and she was smiling through her tears. "I am Ethne," she said. "They call me the Knight of the Sparrow. My family let me keep my house sigil, at least." She shrugged, smiling sadly.

"I am F-Fionn," Fionn answered, suddenly overwhelmed with nerves. She gazed at the tearstained knight and thought her gray eyes were fierce and beautiful. She was distracted to speechlessness for a moment. She shook her head and brought herself back to reality. "I am Fionn, and I have been a sister here in the temple since I was six summers old."

The knight frowned. "Really? What a pity."

It was Fionn's turn to frown. "What do you mean?"

The knight waved a hand. "There's a whole big world out there, my lady. And you've missed it. You haven't seen it."

Fionn hugged herself, thinking of the attack on Tuinhold. "I have seen it," she said darkly. "It is full of anger and fire and violence. There is nothing more to see—"

"Oh, but there is so much more," said the knight, shaking her head.

"I am safe here," Fionn insisted, speaking to her knees, trying to convince herself.

The knight smiled. "Are you?"

Fionn caught the knight's eye and her lashes fluttered: the woman was looking at her with lust again, but as before, there was a softness to her gaze that wasn't threatening whatsoever, no matter her teasing. Fionn felt an odd sort of giddiness come over her and she giggled.

The knight perked up a little, as if she enjoyed the sound of Fionn's laugh. "Oh, you like it when I flirt, do you? You are surprisingly naughty for a sister of the cloth—"

"I am not!" Fionn gasped, though she was still giggling.

"Oh, you're a bad girl, all right," said Ethne, gazing at Fionn with soft admiration. "I wonder how many sisters you have lain with, you naughty thing."

"I-I have never . . ." stammered Fionn, blushing hard. She shyly angled her lashes down and twirled a strand of hair around her finger. When she looked up again, the knight was gazing at her in surprise.

"You mean you've never . . . with anyone? Not even the other sisters?" the knight prompted in amazement.

Fionn shyly shook her head and hugged herself, her eyes down again. She suddenly felt small and childish compared to this worldly knight, who had probably seen and done things she couldn't even imagine. No matter how she protested, Ethne was right: she *had* missed out on a great deal of life's pleasures while hidden away in the temple.

"I've never even been k-kissed," Fionn whispered sadly. She must've sounded sadder than she'd meant to, for the knight asked in soft sympathy, "Would you like to rectify that?"

Fionn looked up. The woman was gazing at her with soft desire again. Heart pounding in her ears, Fionn felt paralyzed as the strong knight took her by her waist and lifted her onto her lap. The woman had moved her as easily as if she were a little doll, and she stared up at her with large eyes, amazed by her strength. The arousal was pumping even harder between her thighs.

The knight had sat Fionn in her lap so that Fionn was facing away from her. She was wondering how they would ever kiss in such an awkward position when the knight gently lifted in Fionn's chin so that Fionn was gazing up at her, and then, after glancing at Fionn's lips, Ethne leaned down over her shoulder and kissed her tenderly.

Fionn moaned, lashes fluttering as she was startled by how good it felt, how strong and commanding the knight's lips were as they tasted her . . . and yet so gentle and inquisitive. As they were kissing, the knight's hands smoothed over Fionn's body and closed over her breasts through the linen of her under-robe.

Fionn's breasts were large and supple, standing young and high behind her linen under-robe. She blushed brightly as her breasts were groped for the first time, blushed and trembled in shock of how good it felt. The knight was gentle and careful, softly massaging her, so that she felt her clitoris pumping fast between her thighs.

She wondered what was happening to her. This wasn't at all like what she'd seen in the streets of Tuinhold! There was no pain, no fear, no weapons, and Ethne wasn't cruel or rough – she was gentle and sweet, often stopping to see if Fionn wanted her to continue, often catching Fionn's eye to see if she was uncomfortable or afraid.

But Fionn suddenly felt fearless. She took the knight's hands and placed one on her breast and the other on her sex, over the fabric. She was not wearing panties beneath – sisters did not wear panties – and she giggled at Ethne's shock when her hand slid under and found only soft thighs and pubic hair. Then it happened: Ethne touched her sex. The knight's careful fingers searched through the nest of her curly yellow hair and found her fat little clitoris, which had been pumping wild for several minutes now.

Fionn melted against Ethne when her clitoris was massaged, gently stroked back and forth between the knight's index finger and thumb. She stared blankly into space as the pleasure mounted, as the first ecstasy overcame her, and when she glanced up, it was to find Ethne looking down at her with hungry eyes, a soft fire blazing in her gaze.

Fionn's heart leapt. She was beautiful and she was desired, and this strong, fierce knight wanted her. Only her! Her thighs trembled as the knight fingered get gently toward stronger, harder arousal, and as her head fell back in a pleasant daze against Ethne's shoulder, the knight carefully untied her rope belt and pulled her under-robe off over her head, tossing it away, so that she was now sitting naked in Ethne's lap.

When Fionn glanced down, the rigid phallus of Ethne's strap was standing erect between her thighs. It had always been there, but it had been covered by the length of Fionn's under-robe. With the under-robe gone, she could see it now. It was dark and appeared to be made of an animal skin. With fluttering lashes, she touched it and was surprised by how firm and yet soft it was. Her small fingers closed experimentally around it.

Ethne, in a daze of lust, feverishly kissed Fionn's naked shoulder, then her neck, then she turned Fionn's face to hers and kissed passionately at her mouth, groping at her breasts and curling her fingers deeper in Fionn's sex. Fionn trembled with pleasure, caught in Ethne's strong grasp and feeling weaker and yet more aroused by the minute.

"Your pussy is so wet," Ethne moaned in Fionn's ear. "I think you're ready."

Fionn blinked. "Ready for what?"

Ethne took Fionn by the hips and lifted her up – then down on the erect phallus. Fionn's eyes grew round as the phallus slowly filled her. She cried out more loudly than she intended, and panicking, Ethne quickly closed her hand over Fionn's mouth. With her other hand, she clutched Fionn's round hip, and gently guided her into gyrating her hips.

Fionn moaned in helpless delight behind Ethne's hand as the pleasure throbbed in her sex. The phallus was plunging deeper and stronger up and up through her clenching walls, and she could feel her sex moistening with each thrust. It took her a moment to realize Ethne was thrusting her hips, even as she guided Fionn's into gyrating. The knight's hard, strong body felt good against Fionn's back as she moved against her, giving her such pleasures as she had never before dreamed.

Fionn placed her small hand over Ethne's, a silent promise that she would no longer scream, and when Ethne had removed her hand from

Fionn's mouth, the little priestess leaned back and kissed Ethne eagerly on the lips. As they kissed, Fionn wiggled her little lips, and Ethne continued thrusting, so that the phallus plunged in and out between the clenching lips of her sex, until the lips were dripping moisture, until Fionn was moaning breathlessly behind their kiss.

Before long, Fionn was bouncing in Ethne's lap, her big breasts flapping, her pretty eyes staring in blank astonishment into the distance as the pleasure mounted. Ethne clutched Fionn's great breasts in both hands and thrusted so deep and hard, Fionn opened her mouth to scream as she climaxed. Ethne was quick, however: she covered Fionn's mouth yet again, and the little priestess shivered in the knight's strong arm as her sex clenched and she released her passion.

Chapter 6

Breakfast in the temple the following morning was an interesting affair. Ava, Lysa, and the knights took breakfast in the great hall with the sisters and their knights. They were given their own table with Ceana, but for some reason Ava couldn't fathom, one of the sisters had decided to sit with them. Her name was Fionn, and she was the sister who was often accompanied by Ceana around the temple. Rather than sitting beside Ceana, however, she sat beside Ethne, who was sitting across from Ceana and Liadan. Ceana kept glaring across the table at Ethne, and for some reason, little blonde Fionn blushed bright as an apple every time she did.

Ethne, however, seemed unbothered. She was too busy glaring hatred at Lysa, Rowan, and Saoirse. Rowan was seated beside Ethne, and Lysa was sitting in Rowan's lap, which seemed to upset Ethne greatly. Ava couldn't understand why, especially when Lysa had sat on Rowan's lap many times in the past. She had also sat on Liadan's lap!

Saoirse was sitting beside Rowan and Lysa and kept feeding them both from her plate. She would scoop a spoonful of oatmeal and feed it lovingly to Rowan, or pick a slice of bread from her plate and place it on Lysa's playfully waiting tongue. Ethne watched this and seethed, while – unbeknownst to her – Fionn watched Ethne in great sympathy.

The only one behaving in a remotely normal manner that morning was Liadan, who was her usual serious self, though very peaceful and happy as well, smiling more often and giving Ava doting looks that made her heart melt. They had made love for hours the night before.

Liadan had surprised Ava with her new strap, a phallic device covered in sheepskin. It was the first time Ava had ever been penetrated by such a device, and after watching how greatly Lysa had enjoyed riding Ethne's strap, she had been eager to ride Liadan's. The big barbarian had not disappointed her, lifting Ava easily up and down on the sheepskin phallus until her sex burst between her trembling thighs.

"So your plan," said Ceana, breaking Ava's lusty thoughts, "is to travel to a temple so the girl can have this child? Why not stay here? You said it yourself, Liadan: the girl's father isn't even looking for her!"

Ava clenched her teeth and paused over her bowl of oatmeal, spoon in hand. Ceana had been referring to Ava as "the girl" all morning and had done the same the evening before, as if she refused to acknowledge her presence at all. Ava had been ignoring it for Liadan's sake, but this morning she had just about had enough.

"We cannot stay here, Ceana," said Liadan firmly. "The king is ignoring us for the time being, yes. But what will happen once he learns of our child? He might perceive it as a threat and send men to kill her! Kill us! This little temple could not withstand the king's men. Many would die senselessly."

Ceana tightened her lips and had no argument, though she seemed bitterly unhappy that Liadan was going to leave. It was so painfully obvious to Ava that Ceana wanted her sister and missed her dearly, but Liadan was so focused on protecting Ava and their child that she wasn't seeing it – yet another reason for Ceana to despise Ava.

"Where, then, shall you go?" Ceana asked heavily.

"What about one of the old temples in Elloris?" suggested Rowan.

"Elloris?" repeated Liadan. "The old elven realm?"

Ava liked the idea. Elloris was an ancient land that had been abandoned since the disappearance of the elves one thousand years before. There were many places to hide there, for the realm was quite large and one could easily become lost within and remain undiscovered for decades. There were also so many protection spells over the old buildings that many were still standing in-tact. When Ava said this and looked eagerly at Liadan, she could see the knight's eyes relenting.

"I agree, it isn't a bad idea," Liadan said.

"So you will go running off to some ancient elven temple because the girl tells you to?" complained Ceana and shook her head.

Ava's nostrils flared. "The *girl's* name is Princess Ava," she said loudly, and the table went still. She straightened up, gazing steadily at Ceana as she said through her teeth, "Future queen of Illa and the seven realms, heir to the mighty House Damaris, and *your* sovereign. You will show me the proper respect by addressing me as such."

"Or?" prompted Ceana, who was sitting very still, calmly regarding Ava.

"Or *I don't know what will happen to you*," Ava returned darkly. From the corner of her eye, she could see Liadan trying not to smile.

To Ava's surprise, Ceana's brows went up. She was impressed. Her eyes went to Liadan. "You know, little sister," she said, "I was worried *Princess Ava* was too soft and weak and *selfish* to take care of you."

Ave tensed.

"But now I see you shall be just fine," Ceana finished and returned to her oatmeal.

The tension seemed to break around the table, and everyone returned to their meals. When Ava glanced up, it was to find Liadan looking down at her with something like pride. She leaned over and whispered very low, "I thought you would stab Ceana in the eye with your spoon! I've never been so proud to call you my woman!"

Ava blushed happily and returned to her oatmeal with a haughty jerk of her chin that made Liadan chuckle.

And so it was settled: they would ride for Elloris and there find a temple for Ava to give birth. That morning, the knights donned their armor, and Ava sadly tucked away her white wedding gown in Liadan's saddlebags, pulling on instead the torn blue traveling gown she had been wearing since her escape from Caradin. "You shall wear it again,"

Liadan had promised her, "when we are wed again on our anniversary." Why was Liadan so sweet? Ava had pulled the towering knight near and kissed her.

To Ava's delight, Rowan and Saoirse had volunteered to accompany them to Elloris. Saoirse explained that she was concerned for their safety, for the forests of Elloris were full of orcs and goblins, and such creatures would be attracted to Ava's dragon egg. They would come in droves to take it. When Ava asked why, she was shocked to learn that orcs and goblins enjoyed eating dragons.

Mother Tiede bid them a sweet farewell, loading them down with free bread, dried meat, and milk, and with their new knapsacks and bundles, they gathered on the step to say their final goodbyes to Ceana.

It was a cold wintry morning, though the sky was bright blue over the land, and a steady breeze lifted their hair. Birds were singing, and the sound lifted Ava's spirits. She was still giddy from the night's festivities. Liadan had danced with her so merrily, she couldn't stop thinking of it. She hadn't known Liadan could dance!

Ceana and Mother Tiede stood on the step, gazing down at the group as morning sunlight stretched pale fingers over them.

"Take care of my baby sister, Princess Ava, future queen of Illa and the seven realms," said Ceana, surprising Ava with her playfulness.

Ava was clutching Liadan's arm and lifted her chin regally as she answered, "I shall always take care of my sweet Liadan! You take care and be here when we return to visit!"

Ceana seemed pleased by Ava's answer and surprised Ava further by bowing deeply to her. When she had straightened up again, she looked at Liadan and said, "I am unhappy to know my niece shall be brought up so far away in an elven temple and not in the land of our blood. Do bring her to visit one of these days."

"I shall," Liadan answered.

Ava felt guilty to hear Ceana's words, but she knew they had to hide in elven lands because it was the safest option at the moment. A temple was also ideal because such places were holy ground, blessed by the gods themselves, their blessing reinforced by the prayers of ancient priestesses.

All priestesses were granted the power of healing and blessing by the gods. Such had been the way since the dawn of time. Even among the Wildoras, the priestesses could heal wounds through prayer. And so, Ava was delighted when Fionn, the little blonde priestess, came bursting out the temple doors, knapsack in hand, and begged to accompany them.

Ceana and Mother Tiede looked around at Fionn in shock.

Standing there in her simple red robe, Mother Tiede was a very tall, stiff, and dignified woman, so seeing her lose her composure almost made Ava giggle. The Mother's eyes about popped from her head when Fionn announced her departure.

"You shall do no such thing!" Mother Tiede cried, completely appalled.

"I shall!" little Fionn wailed – so defiantly that Mother Tiede gasped in shock.

Not only was Fionn carrying a knapsack, but she was also wrapped in a fur traveling cloak against the cold. She ran down the steps with her red robes flying behind her, and to everyone's surprise, she threw herself against Ethne. The Knight of the Sparrow caught Fionn against her and looked around guiltily.

Ceana's lips tightened. She was incensed. Ava gasped when the temple knight's hand went immediately to her sword hilt. "Just as I suspected! You fucked Fionn, you—!"

Liadan looked irritably at Ethne. "Shite. Did you really?"

Still holding Fionn in her arms (as Fionn gazed up at her dotingly), Ethne shrugged and gave a wincing smile.

"SLAY HER!" Mother Tiede bellowed, her eyes popping like a frog. "SLAY THEM BOTH!"

Ava was shocked by the woman's rage, and even more shocked when Ceana drew her sword to obey.

Behind Ava, she heard the *ching* of blades being drawn in retaliation, and when she glanced back, Rowan, Saoirse, and Lysa had all grimly drawn their weapons – though Lysa looked as if she might stab Ethne, not Ceana.

Liadan had also drawn her blade. It blazed with fire as she took a protective step in front of Ethne. Ceana's blade was glowing with the same golden flame. She looked down the step at Liadan regretfully.

"Step aside, Liadan," Ceana said heavily. "It is the law, and I must obey. Ethne and Fionn both must die. For once, do not be dragged into the messes of your cowardly friends!"

"Sister, please!" Liadan said through her teeth. "Do not make me raise a blade against thee!"

Ceana's hand shook on her sword, and she hesitated. Her blue eyes, so like Liadan's, were relenting.

Mother Tiede's nostrils flared. "Do your duty, knight!" she barked at Ceana. "Or your life will be forfeit as well!"

Having made her decision, Ceana reluctantly brought her blade down on Liadan in a quick arc, slashing her own sister in a toss of blood.

"No!" Ava screamed in horror, but Ceana only grazed Liadan's greave as her flaming sword came around, and instead of running Liadan through, she shoved her sister out of the way. Liadan grunted in pain as she fell to the snow, and Ava, tears in her eyes, fell to her knees and hugged Liadan around the shoulders. When she looked up, it was to see Ceana lunging down the stair at Ethne, as behind her, Mother Tiede folded her hands and watched with calm satisfaction.

"No!" Lysa screamed angrily. "Leave her alone!"

Ethne hugged Fionn tight, and as Fionn sobbed wildly, the knight tried to pull them back from the swing of Ceana's flaming blade, but she didn't need to: an arrow zipped past Ethne and embedded with a twang in Ceana's shoulder. Blood spattered as Ceana gasped, eyes blank with pain, and tumbled down the step, falling at the bottom in a heap.

Tears in her eyes as she clutched Liadan, Ava looked around and realized Saoirse had fired her bow. The tall blonde knight slowly lowered her weapon and stood grim and powerful, glaring up the step at Mother Tiede and silently daring her to call more knights. Mother Tiede, thinking better of it, bitterly glared at Saoirse and lifted her chin.

"Sister!" Liadan sobbed, staring aghast at her sister's crumpled body.

"It's a flesh wound, she's alive," said Rowan, who came quickly to Liadan and – shocking Ava – lifted the big knight over her shoulder like a doll. Liadan was injured and bleeding from her leg where Ceana had struck her, and as she hung helplessly over Rowan's shoulder, tears filled her eyes. She was still staring at her sister's body.

"Move!" Rowan snarled, pulling a dazed Ava to her feet by the arm. She looked at Ethne and Fionn, who were both standing in shock (Fionn was still sobbing) and snarled, "I said move! Stand not amazed! Saoirse has bought us time before that old hag sics the whole town on us!"

Mother Tiede's breasts heaved at the insult. "Yes, run!" she mocked, her vicious eyes narrowed. "Run for your lives! And if you ever set foot in Hastow again, I'll have the lot of you slain!"

And so, they ran. Saoirse and Rowan were the only ones with horses, and so they headed fast into town and purchased new horses for the rest of the party. By the time they were all mounted up and riding toward the road, they could hear the knights of the temple galloping after them, while the townspeople stood gawping in the streets.

With the gold from Queen Saraid's tomb, Ava had bought Liadan and herself a fine chestnut stallion, but they could not ride it together. Liadan was too injured to mount and sit a horse without aid, and as a result, had wound up sharing a saddle with Rowan, the only one in the group strong enough to hold her up with ease. Rowan was, after all, more than six feet tall and likely half-giant to boot.

Lysa had purchased herself a small, quick mare, its black coat glossy in the pale winter sunlight, and Ethne had purchased a brown stallion for herself and Fionn to share.

And so, they rode hard down the road, Saoirse in the lead on her great golden stallion, and a horde of angry temple knights riding hot after them.

Ava knew how to ride a horse and it was, in fact, the only thing she had bothered to learn aside from reading. She secretly prided herself that she was actually quite good at it, and it was with ease that she kept her horse just behind Saoirse and also beside Rowan, who was holding an injured Liadan upright in the saddle.

Liadan didn't look well, and fear gripped Ava's heart. The Knight of the Wild was pale from having lost much blood (Liadan had attempted to walk while they were purchasing horses, causing more blood flow), and she was in a daze, her head rolling on her neck. Rowan seemed determined to keep her from passing out and shook Liadan often while cursing under her breath.

Ava's heart was thudding in her ears. She was terrified. It seemed that in only a matter of seconds, things had gone to hell. One moment they were saying their pleasant farewells to Ceana and the next moment Saoirse was shooting her in Ethne's defense. Where was Saoirse leading them, and would they make it there alive? The temple knights were not slowing down or letting up.

After several minutes of anxious riding, Saoirse surprised Ava when she slowed her horse, falling back to ride between Ava and Rowan. Saoirse was more hard-faced and grim than ever, and whatever she was about to say, Ava knew it wouldn't be pleasant.

"There's an old cabin to the east just up ahead!" Saoirse called over the roar of galloping hooves. "I want you to lead them there and wait for me—"

"I shall *not* leave you alone to face an entire horde!" Rowan growled at once.

Saoirse blinked impatiently. "Dammit, Rowan! Do as I say!"

Rowan didn't answer, instead grabbing Saoirse's arm, pulling her near, and kissing her hard on the mouth, even as their horses kept desperately galloping. When the lovers had parted, Saoirse gave Ava a grim nod, then turned her great stallion about, drawing her bow as she galloped off.

Ava thought she saw tears behind Rowan's eyes, but the big knight charged her horse ahead before Ava could really tell.

As Saoirse had commanded, Rowan led them east into the trees, and as they turned off the road, Ava could hear the sounds of battle. Women were screaming and falling (for all the temple knights were women), and horses were braying, boots were crunching over the snow. Ava thought she heard Saoirse cry out in pain and her heart quickened. She told herself not Saoirse, not Saoirse, not the greatest instructor to mentor at the academy, not the woman who had once slain a hundred orcs single-handedly, or so the stories said. Saoirse had faced greater odds.

There was a cabin back in the trees as Saoirse had claimed. It was small and lopsided, as if the roof were weakening. Spidery trees and bushes pressed around it, smothering it on all sides, and an old well stood layered in snow in the front yard.

They dismounted quickly, and Rowan rushed Liadan inside the cabin, carrying the big delirious knight in both arms.

Inside, the single-room cabin was dark and cold. There was a hearth, a few cracked cauldrons, wooden chairs, and a straw pallet lay against one wall. An old wooden table also sat in the corner, under a window with a cracked and frosty pane.

Rowan went at once to the straw pallet and gently laid Liadan on it. Ava practically threw herself on her knees beside Liadan, gazing into her face. The Knight of the Wild was barely conscious and was feverish too boot. Little beads of sweat were gathering on her brow, and her red hair was damp and stringy. She was muttering words that made no sense, and whenever she opened her eyes and looked at Ava, it was as if she couldn't really see her.

"What's the *matter* with her?" Ava moaned.

"She was cut by no ordinary blade, my lady," said Rowan heavily. "Ceana is a magi like her sister. A cut from her is like poison."

"Gods be good," Ava breathed, tears rising to blind her. "We must do something!"

"I can help," said a small voice behind Ava. "Let me help."

Ava looked up. Fionn was hovering nearby. Her face was wet with tears, and she was wringing her small hands, but her pale blue eyes seemed determined.

"You've caused us enough trouble," snarled Rowan, who was standing over Liadan like a grim guardian. She stepped protectively forward, blocking Fionn's path.

"Let her help, for the sake of the gods, Rowan!" Ethne snapped.

Ethne was distraught and disheveled. She had been staring miserably at Liadan, but hearing Rowan, she turned her eyes to the Black Lioness and glared.

Without warning, Rowan leapt on Ethne and slammed her into the wall. Everyone watched, paralyzed with shock, as Rowan slammed her forearm against Ethne's neck and pulled a dagger, placing the tip of the blade just under Ethne's chin.

"Stop this madness!" Lysa shrieked, looking as if she would lunge on Rowan and pry her off. Her entire body was tense.

Rowan ignored Lysa. "Saoirse will perish because of you, after one night – one night! – of having been my wife!" she hissed at Ethne in a low, deadly voice. "I should drive this blade through your wretched face and be done with it!"

"Then do it," Ethne whispered. She stood against the wall, unmoving, tears in her eyes. She was weeping for Liadan, and Ava knew in that moment that she felt guilty for what had happened to her friend. She was welcoming death. Ava felt badly for her. She wanted to be angry with Ethne as the others were, but it was difficult when she knew just how heartbroken Ethne was over Lysa and the reason she had likely bedded Fionn.

For one horrible second, it seemed as if Rowan would indeed slay Ethne right then and there.

Lysa stepped forward. "Enough of this, Rowan! Unhand her!"

To Ava's surprise, Rowan listened to Lysa this time. She blinked angrily, then shoved herself away from Ethne, and roughly sheathing her dagger on her belt again, she stomped to the door and outside. The door slammed behind her so hard, Ava flinched.

Ethne remained against the wall. She did not meet Lysa's furious gaze.

Ava thought Lysa looked as if she wanted to stab Ethne as much as Rowan did. Instead, the former handmaiden turned to Fionn and said roughly, "Well? Are you going to heal Liadan? Or are you only good for one thing?"

Fionn's cheeks blushed brightly, and her face was tight with anger, but she ignored Lysa and turned to Liadan, kneeling beside her where she lay, moaning and shaking, on the straw pallet.

"Please, help her!" Ava whispered. She was still kneeling near Liadan's head, and her small hand was stroking the dazed knight's tangled red hair.

"I shall do what I can, my lady," answered Fionn kindly.

As Ava watched, Fionn bowed her head, closed her eyes, and folded her hands in prayer. She began speaking words Ava did not understand, but she had heard them before. There had been a priestess back at Caradin, old Mother Roisin, who had prayed often over sick servants and injured knights. She had spoken the same words Fionn was speaking now. It was an ancient tongue, known only to the order of priestesses.

As Fionn prayed, Ava could see the color returning to Liadan's cheeks and lips. Her fever was also abating. Before long, Liadan was sleeping deeply and breathing easier, no longer was she shaking, and the cut on her leg had stopped bleeding. The blood ran dry and then . . . disappeared!

Ava looked across at Fionn in wonder. The little priestess had finished praying, and when she lifted her face and opened her eyes, her cheeks were glowing with heat, her eyes were bright and shimmering. She looked beautiful in an ethereal sense. Utterly beautiful. Ava stared at her. So did Ethne and Lysa, who hovered near.

Ethne was silently doting on Fionn, and seeing this, Ava thought Lysa looked a little envious and hateful. The former handmaiden folded her arms and muttered, "So you're good for more than tongue-fucking after all . . ." as she walked away to the window and peered out.

Hearing Lysa's words, Fionn blushed angrily but did not respond. Instead, she looked at Ava and said, "It is done, my lady. We should allow her to sleep for a few hours here. She will need to rest for the wound to heal completely."

"A few hours?" repeated Ethne weakly. "Those mad temple knights might come here before long."

Ava sighed. She didn't know what to do. They couldn't move Liadan, and they couldn't hope to fight off dozens of angry knights alone.

"She's back!" cried Lysa in great relief. She was still looking out the window and her eyes were bright with happiness.

Ethne looked around at Lysa, then ran to the door and yanked it open. Standing outside in the snow, kissing on the step, where Rowan and Saoirse. Saoirse was bloody, disheveled, and exhausted, but she laughed as Rowan playfully kissed her all over her face.

Ava saw Ethne tighten angrily when Lysa ran past her out into the snow, ran down the step, and leapt on Saoirse and Rowan, who laughed and embraced her. The three stood on the step exchanging playful kisses, and Ethne watched them, her hands shaking. Eventually, Ethne snapped the door shut and turned, stomped into the room, and sat in an old wooden chair. She folded her arms and said nothing.

Ava knew that the person Ethne needed most in the moment was Liadan, but Liadan was sleeping and too ill to support her. And so, knowing that she was the next best thing, Ava left Fionn to watch over Liadan and crossed the room to Ethne, who did not look up from her brooding.

"I know it is hard, seeing Lysa behave so . . . loosely," Ava said soothingly. She didn't know how else to put it, but Lysa was indeed sleeping around a shocking amount. Back at the temple of Eyslath, Ethne wasn't the only one who had bedded a priestess, she was just the only one who was caught. Ava had accidentally walked in on Lysa sleeping with two young sisters in her bed. All three had been naked.

"How else should I feel?" Ethne said tonelessly and stared darkly into space. She was sitting with her arms folded, her knees spread. She looked as if she was pouting, and it might have been comical – a big, strong knight poo-pooing like a child—if not for the circumstances.

"Lysa loves you, Ethne," Ava said gently, "she's just not . . . *in* love with you. You must move on. I never thought I'd say this, but I can't stand to see you like this."

Ethne laughed tonelessly. "My thanks, my lady . . . I suppose."

Ava laughed guiltily. "What I mean is, I didn't like you much in the beginning. I was convinced you would hurt Lysa, that you would use her and cast her aside. Seems like things have happened in a backward way I can't fully grasp."

"Me neither, princess, rest assured," said Ethne with another humorless laugh. "But perhaps I deserve it. I have broken many hearts, lain with many women who thought I would make a match of them, only to abandon them. Mairin was mad, but she was right to be hurt by my doings. I whispered such sweet nothings in her ear, then I robbed her of her coin purse, and when she sent me letters asking me to run away with her, I ignored them. I abandoned her after promising, *promising* to never leave." Her eyes went to Fionn, who had been listening in shock, and she said miserably, "I deserve for dear Lysa to use me and cast me aside. And I don't deserve sweet Fionn's love."

"That is not true!" said Fionn, bouncing up from Liadan's side. She came across the room, hair streaming, and sat on Ethne's knee. "That is not true at all!"

Ethne smiled sadly at Fionn, placing a careful gauntlet on her narrow waist.

"Everyone has a past," Fionn insisted, "and no one is without sin! You are a good woman at heart, I know it! You just need a good woman to steady you! Lysa is not faithful and true. I hath studied her long, and she is not the right woman for you!"

"Are you the right woman for me?" asked Ethne, quite pleased by Fionn's passionate little speech. She stared at Fionn intently, and the little priestess became flustered under her steady gaze. Ava didn't blame her: Ethne's gaze could be quite intense.

"I . . . that is . . ." said Fionn, blushing prettily and looking down.

"And are you a sinner?" continued Ethne, highly amused. "How many men have you slain? How many children have you dashed against walls? Have you stolen? Have you raped? I doubt one so pure as you could ever conceive of sinning."

"But I *have* sinned," Fionn sadly insisted and hugged herself in shame. "I lay with you – in the temple of my goddess, no less! At the very shrine! Ceana was right to attempt my execution—!"

"What horse shite is that!" cried Ethne, amazed. "Why should it be a *sin* that you should lay with me? I honestly doubt Eyslath gave a shite. She probably watched and pleasured herself."

Fionn gasped and blushed right to her hairline.

Ava giggled behind her hand. "Ethne! You'll give the poor thing a heart attack!"

Fionn's lashes coyly angled down and she giggled. "I confess, I do like it when you talk dirty," she said, making Ethne smile.

"Ava likes it as well, don't you, Ava?" said Ethne. She reached up, grabbed Ava gently at the waist, and pulled her down on her other knee, so that Ava and Fionn were facing each other. As Fionn watched with large eyes, Ethne groped hard at Ava's heavy breast, caressing through her gown, and Ava gasped and giggled, playfully smacking Ethne's hand away. Ethne kissed Ava's neck and cheek, making her blush.

"Stop that!" Ava scolded, and Ethne smiled and stopped her kisses. Instead, Ethne kissed Fionn's neck and cheek, and Fionn giggled happily, blushing when one of her heavy breasts was groped this time. Ethne became a little carried away, Ava thought, almost as if she had forgotten Ava was there, and the Knight of the Sparrow kissed Fionn passionately yet gently on the lips. Fionn looked as if she would melt in her ecstasy.

"Are you my woman, then?" Ethne asked, looking intently at Fionn again. Her voice was soft and intimate. She kissed Fionn's neck and cheek over and over. "Shall you be mine? Truly mine?" she whispered between kisses.

"Y-Yes," said Fionn, shivering under the fervent kisses, then gazing at Ethne with breathless longing. She blushed again as she spoke, and her pale lashes fluttered. Ava gazed at her, thinking she was so small and delicate and pretty – no wonder Lysa hated her. She wondered what was under Fionn's shapeless red robe. Fionn must've had a beautiful body for Ethne to be so quickly smitten.

Pleased by Fionn's answer, Ethne leaned close and kissed her slowly on the lips. Fionn was shivering from the kiss when Ethne pulled away, and she looked so happy, Ava thought she would faint.

"Shall we make love again?" Fionn whispered excitedly. "Shall Ava join us?" She looked at Ava with hungry blue eyes.

Ava gasped, scandalized.

Ethne chuckled. "I knew you were a naughty little thing." She gazed past Fionn at Liadan, who lay sleeping on the pallet, sunlight streaming over her through the window, and her expression grew somber. "Perhaps when Liadan has awoken, we shall make a foursome of it. Li and I always share our women."

Ava's heart fluttered. She was excited at the prospect of sleeping with sweet, pretty Fionn, but she also knew doing so would infuriate Lysa, who was – she and Ethne both knew – in love with Ava. Ava looked at Ethne and suspected the Sparrow Knight wanted the foursome out of bitter revenge. She did not look forward to the drama later.

Before Ava could voice her suspicions, however, Lysa, Rowan, and Saoirse returned from the front step, looking flushed and happy from their reunion. There was still much bitterness and anger between everyone, for Ethne glared at Rowan, Rowan glared at Ethne, and Lysa glared *daggers* when she saw little Fionn sitting on Ethne's knee, to which Fionn blushed and shrank. The only one devoid of anger and jealousy was Saoirse, who pulled up a chair beside Ethne and started discussing their next move with a very businesslike air. Lysa perched on Saoirse's knee, but she was hardly paying attention to the conversation at hand, instead glaring angrily and steadily at Fionn, who avoided her eye.

"If we are really venturing all the way to Elloris," Saoirse said to the room at large, "we shall need to take a ship across the *Silia*. We could return to Hargendon and acquire a ship at the port there, but that would mean going past Hastow again. The risk is too great."

"Adwean is nearer anyway," said Rowan, who loomed beside Saoirse's chair, arms crossed, great hammer and shield on her back.

"What? No!" said Ethne at once, sitting straight up, as if someone had poked her. Everyone looked at her, and she added, "Adwean is my hometown. We can't go there! I was exiled!"

"So we'll put a bag over your head," mocked Lysa, arms folded. She was looking at Ethne as if she wanted to stab her. Her glaring eyes went back to Fionn, then to Ethne's face, and her lip trembled with hurt.

Ava thought Lysa was being a massive hypocrite after all the sleeping around she'd done at the temple only the night before.

"You don't understand," snarled Ethne at Lysa. "I was ordered never to return on pain of death! People were very angry about what I'd done. There's an entire house in Adwean that would like to see my head mounted over their hearth."

"As I'm sure there are everywhere," returned Lysa dismissively.

Rowan stared a long time at Ethne in disbelief, and her eyes narrowed. "Are you *jesting?*" she demanded. "You're wanted in all seven realms now! It doesn't matter where you go at this point – someone will be after you!"

Ethne glared at Rowan. "You know damn-well it would be h-hard for me to go back there—!"

"What other choice do we have, Ethne?" Saoirse asked quietly. "We must away to Elloris."

"Before you make more mischief for us," added Rowan darkly.

Ethne glared at Rowan and snapped, "Fine!"

Ava had the feeling Ethne wanted to get up and storm out, but Ava and Fionn were sitting on her knees, and not wanting to shove them off, she tensed instead, her hands nicely tightening on their waists.

When it looked as if Ethne wasn't going to continue her protests, Saoirse looked toward Liadan with concern and said heavily, "Then it's settled. We shall rest here and let Liadan recover. Then we head to Adwean. And from there, it is away to Elloris."

Chapter 7

As Liadan slept peacefully on the straw pallet, Rowan and Saoirse built up a fire over the hearth, and everyone else rolled out their bedrolls near the flames. They all laid down to rest there in the gloomy cabin, and because Ethne and Lysa were now angry with each other, Lysa had nowhere to sleep, for Ethne was now sharing her bedroll with Fionn. With Liadan still sleeping on the straw pallet, Ava had plenty of room in her bedroll and invited Lysa to join her. The little handmaiden gratefully climbed in beside the princess and lay on her back, staring at the ceiling in contemplation.

Before long, the room was full of the sound of soft breathing as Liadan, Ethne, and Fionn slept. Rowan and Saoirse, however, lay awake, speaking together in low voices of the journey to come. They were nearest the door, so as to defend the others from attack, while Ava and Lysa lay in their bedroll near Liadan.

Ava decided to take the opportunity to interrogate Lysa about her wild behavior, not only because she wished to defend Ethne but also because . . . she was curious. Lysa was having more sex than a sailor at port!

"Lysa?" Ava whispered.

"Hmm?" returned Lysa sleepily. She was still lying on her back, gazing thoughtfully at the stained ceiling.

"Why are you doing this to Ethne?"

Lysa scowled. "Doing what?"

"You know what! Sleeping around," Ava scolded. "Ethne loves you and—"

"I don't believe it!" Lysa cried, sitting up on her elbow. "You're on Ethne's side now? Why?"

Ava sighed unhappily. "It's just, Ethne is a good woman and you're hurting her. I see it now."

Lysa snorted. "Ethne is *not* a good woman, nor is she true! Do you know how many tavern wenches she did bed back in Hargendon?"

"Only because she thought you didn't want her," Ava returned, still scolding. "The way you carry on with Rowan and Saoirse! Why? You know it hurts her."

"Does it? I didn't think she cared. Look at her and that little . . .waif." So saying, Lysa waved a disgusted hand at Fionn, who was sleeping happily on Ethne's breastplate as the knight held her close.

"I suspect she slept with Fionn after she saw you dancing with Rowan and Saoirse at the feast," said Ava. "And I know you slept with them afterward, as well as those two priestesses."

Lysa gasped. "Ava! *Goddess.* How came you to spy upon me so? It was your wedding night! Shouldn't you have been off with Liadan?"

"Liadan and I wanted to get you in our bed. I went to look for you twice and both times you were with others."

"Oh," whispered Lysa sheepishly.

"You are so careless with Ethne's heart yet want to play the victim when she doth move on. I never knew you could be so . . . vicious."

Lysa sighed. "You are right, my princess. I didn't know I could be so vicious either. But I'm not in love with Ethne and I don't want to be her lady! I know that now. I keep telling her, and she doth continue to pursue. That is hardly my fault."

"I suppose you're right. At least she has Fionn now."

Lysa's lips tightened angrily. "Yes. Good for her," she said scathingly.

Ava laughed softly. "You don't love Ethne, yet you are jealous of Fionn?"

"Ethne is my first knight!" Lysa cried, keeping her voice low so as not to be heard. "Even if I am no longer with her, why should it please me to watch as another is doted upon by her? If you were to part ways with Liadan, would it please you to see her kissing another woman? Of course, not!"

"No, I suppose not." Ava was silent as she suddenly realized: if Liadan were to love another and kiss her in front of Ava, Ava might lose all dignity and pull someone's hair out. Thankfully, Liadan loved only her. If she lay with other women, it was purely pleasure, and Ava was always a part of it.

"I know it's silly, but in my mind, Ethne shall always be my knight, even if I despise her." Lysa laughed weakly, and her eyes went fondly to Ethne, where she lay sleeping with Fionn.

Ava laughed as well. "The two of you deserve each other."

There was a pause as they both lay on their backs, staring at the ceiling, lost in thought. Then Lysa said very quietly, "There is only one woman I shall ever love. I know that now. Try as I might to move on, to love another . . ."

Ava blushed as Lysa's meaning became clear.

"I know you love Liadan, and I would not get in the way of that," Lysa went on, "but just know that I shall always love you, and I am here if you need me. I would do most anything for you."

Ava smiled sadly. Her heart was fluttering in her chest to hear Lysa's soft-spoken confession. "Oh, sweetest Lysa," she whispered. "Why didn't you ever tell me how you felt before?"

Lysa made a helpless noise. "I am not the sort of woman that doth please you! I am slender and small . . . and ugly."

"You are not ugly!" Ava said indignantly at once.

"I am not big and strong the way you like," Lysa went on. "I cannot lift you up, nor make aggressive love to you. I am not a great warrior like Liadan but a rogue and a sneak. I have no magick. I can barely even read! There is nothing in me you should desire—"

Ava reached over, cupped Lysa's face with one hand, and kissed her on the lips.

"A-Ava!" Lysa whispered, blushing. She was confused but pleased.

"I love you, too," Ava whispered, "as my friend and companion, and there is nothing I wouldn't do for you either. I wish you would stay with me at court once I have taken back Caradin. Be my advisor, sweet Lysa—"

"And watch as you dote on Liadan and have her children? No, thank you."

Ava sighed sadly. "I suppose it is selfish of me to press it."

"It is," Lysa teased.

Ava smiled.

There was a moan from the straw pallet, and Ava looked around to see Liadan had awoken. The Knight of the Wild was blinking, her head turning against the straw. Ava's heart fluttered, and she climbed from the bedroll and up onto the low pallet, where she snuggled in beside Liadan on her belly. Her great breasts sat against Liadan's breastplate, the cleavage swelling from the collar of her blue traveling gown.

"My love!" Ava whispered happily, peering into Liadan's face. "Are you well?"

Liadan blinked sleepily and smiled. She reached up and touched Ava's face, and her eyes were warm with love. Ava's heart melted. She thought she would spend the rest of her life melting when Liadan looked at her.

Liadan kissed Ava softly on the lips and let her head drop again to the straw, moaning hoarsely, "I am well, my love, my darling."

Ava's heart fluttered to hear such sweet words from Liadan's lips. Since their wedding in Hastow, the Knight of the Wild had become more doting, gentle, and sweet than ever, and it was making her deliriously happy.

Liadan glanced around and frowned at her unfamiliar surroundings. "Where are we?"

"An abandoned cabin not far from Hastow," Lysa answered, kneeling near the pallet. She pushed her mousey brown hair behind her ear and glowered as she said, "You were nearly slain thanks to Ethne! That magick blade would have killed thee like poison!"

"Ethne is not to blame, fair Lysa," said Liadan at once. "Ceana was doing as she was bid by her masters, and Ethne—"

"Was being a dog, as usual!" Lysa shrilled.

Liadan laughed. "I suppose nothing much around here has changed," she said to Ava, who laughed as well.

"Of course, you would defend her," scolded Lysa. She glanced sadly over Liadan's body. "But after what happened to you, you should be furious!"

"You are so sweet to worry for me, dear Lysa," Liadan answered, amused. She reached up, grabbed Lysa by the waist, and easily lifted her onto the pallet, so that she, like Ava, was resting on her belly on Liadan's breastplate.

Liadan looked between their faces, her eyes soft. Ava saw her blue eyes graze lustily over her great cleavage, then Liadan looked at Lysa and seemed annoyed that the former handmaiden was wearing a leather chest guard. The guard hid her cleavage completely.

"Things were easier when you wore a gown," complained Liadan, making Lysa blush when she reached back and roughly undid the buckle, pulling the chest guard off over Lysa's head.

"Liadan!" Lysa whispered in soft protest. She was blushing quite hard and glanced around, as if she hoped Rowan and Saoirse hadn't noticed, but her other lovers were not watching or noticing.

Liadan ignored Lysa's whispers and tugged at the smaller woman's tunic, pulling the laces so that her cleavage poured free. And now, like Ava, Lysa's breasts were sitting – swollen together – on Liadan's breastplate. This seemed to satisfy Liadan, who let her head rest again as she observed them.

"You were mine before you lay with Rowan and Saoirse," said Liadan, cupping the back of Lysa's brown hair, "and you were Ethne's before you were mine. Remember that, dear Lysa."

Ava could tell that Lysa was pleased, but Lysa cried out indignantly anyway, "I am not property, Liadan!"

Liadan smiled and shook her head. "That is not what I meant. There is a certain . . .hierarchy to things. It's a rule we made when we used to travel together as girls. Whoever sleeps with a woman always stays her first. If Rowan and Saoirse wanted you right now, I could say no because I had slept with you first. I would be in my rights to draw my blade on them, in fact. And if Ethne woke up right now and said that she wanted you and that I should leave you alone, I would have to surrender you or else fight for you. In our eyes, you shall always belong to Ethne because she had you first."

Lysa was blushing brightly. "You all go on about women as if we were pieces of meat!"

"No, it's just the way of things. The point was to keep us from brawling over our lovers. When knights travel around in groups, we tend to sleep with the same women, and fighting happens, people get hurt," explained Liadan.

"Like today," Lysa miserably admitted.

Liadan raised her brows inquisitively.

"While you were sleeping," explained Ava, "Rowan pulled a blade on Ethne and nearly killed her. Or threatened to, anyway."

Liadan nodded grimly. "That wouldn't have happened if Rowan and Saoirse had respected the code and not bedded you without Ethne's permission, Lysa."

Lysa shook her head. "The four of you are absolutely mad."

Liadan wasn't listening. She was looking at Lysa's breasts. Lysa trembled as Liadan stared at her, and Ava knew she was trembling with anticipation, though she was pretending not to enjoy it.

"Liadan!" Lysa scolded when Liadan tugged on her tunic, pulling it down over her shoulder and causing one of her breasts to pour free.

Clutching the back of Lysa's neck, Liadan pulled her close and kissed her on the mouth. Lysa blushed brightly but frowned and kissed Liadan back.

Ava watched them kissing a moment and felt her sex pumping in her panties. She blushed when Liadan's hand closed hard on her backside, and the next thing she knew, Liadan had pulled her close, so that her breasts were in the Knight of the Wild's face. As Lysa watched, breathless from the kiss, tousled hair in her eyes, Liadan pulled Ava's laces free with her teeth. Ava's heart pounded as her big breasts shivered free, as Lysa watched with hunger, as Liadan's burning eyes grazed over the soft mounds.

Squeezing Ava's backside again, Liadan pulled Ava up, so that her breasts were in Liadan's face, and then Ava gasped in delight when she felt the barbarian's hungry lips sucking hard at her nipple. Ava hugged Liadan's head and stroked her red hair as she was suckled, her soft cries and moans soon filling the room. She frowned against the pleasure and looked around in a daze to find Lysa watching as she was suckled by Liadan, watching with hungry brown eyes.

Without warning, Liadan grabbed Lysa by the backside next, drew her up near so that her breasts were in Liadan's face, and then Liadan was sucking on Lysa's little breast, sucking fast, so that it jiggled as the pink nipple was pulled. Lysa was gasping and moaning, her eyes hooded, her cheeks blushing with shame that Ava was watching. Then Lysa's eyes fluttered open wide, and Ava glanced back and saw that Liadan's hand had slid down the back of Lysa's tight trousers and she was fingering Lysa as she sucked her nipple.

Ava had only seconds to watch before she felt Liadan's fingers in her panties, and then she was being fingered as well. She gasped, holding on to Liadan's head and her soft red hair, arching her back as the barbarian's relentless fingers plunged hard and hungry through her tight, moist walls.

Fingering Ava and Lysa at the same time, Liadan grunted as she took turns sucking their breasts, kissing their necks, tasting their lips, and trapped in her hard, strong arms, they screamed softly as they enjoyed every wet second of it.

Chapter 8

Apparently, Saoirse had slain all the temple knights who had pursued them from Hastow – all twenty-six—leaving a pile of bloody bodies on the snow-swept road in her wake. Lysa was in awe of the woman, as she had been since Hargendon, where Saoirse had slain so many ruffians while climbing the stairs in the Water Hole just to rescue her from Bella. Lysa thought she understood completely why Rowan was in love with Saoirse and had to admit she was a little envious of the newlyweds.

Because Saoirse had successfully defended them, they were able to rest at the abandoned cabin for far more than two hours, and it wasn't until sundown that they set out on horseback for Adwean.

Wearing her leather armor and fur cape, Lysa climbed onto the back of her sleek black mare – which she had named Cherry Blossom—and took off down the road after the others. She was proud of herself for how quickly she was learning to ride and fight. Before long, she would be able to strike out on her own if she wished. But only after she had helped Ava. The quest to destroy the watchtowers sounded like fun, even if it was undeniably dangerous, and Lysa wanted to see Ava become queen of the seven realms. She knew that if she walked away now, she would spend all her time worrying that Ava and Liadan were well, and she would not forgive herself if anything happened to them. She knew she must see the journey through to the end, whatever happened.

As they rode along, Lysa could tell that Ethne was still apprehensive about approaching Adwean, her hometown, from which she had been exiled. And though she tried to deny it, Lysa felt badly for Ethne and wanted to comfort her. She knew now, however, that it was no longer her place to comfort Ethne. Now Ethne had Fionn – the little hussy!

The skinny blonde womanchild sat the saddle before Ethne, giggling when Ethne whispered in her ear, smiling when Ethne sang a soothing song, and sometimes turning in the saddle to kiss Ethne on the cheek. Lysa watched them and hated them, remembering how it was just yesterday – actually yesterday!—that Ethne had whispered and sang and kissed Lysa as they were traveling together. Now she was forgotten so quickly. Ethne didn't even look at her.

Lysa had to suppose it was her own fault. She had consistently pushed Ethne away. She had bedded Saoirse and Rowan again and again while expecting that Ethne would just accept it and always be there. At the time, she hadn't understood the knights' code or that she was causing strife among them. She hadn't understood that Ethne's relationship with Rowan was very different from her relationship with Liadan.

Liadan was Ethne's best friend. They shared everything together, did everything together – even having sex with women. But Rowan was Ethne's rival and they fought over everything and anything. Knowing that now, Lysa regretted causing the rift between them, for rivals though they had been, Ethne and Rowan had still loved each other as sisters. Now they didn't even look at each other.

Lysa didn't know how much longer she could stand traveling with people who all hated each other. She wanted to make things better, perhaps corner Ethne and explain that she hadn't understood the silly "code," but she knew she was helpless to do anything: as the source of the strife, she would only make things worse.

Adwean was only a few hours away, and it was still night when they arrived at the gate of the great city. Here, there were many guards posted, and the city was walled, with men walking the battlements, carrying torches and spears. Adwean was one of the biggest cities in Realm Illa, the home of some of the greatest knights in the tourney. It was the place where the grand tourney was held, and warriors came from as far as Realm Ivorest to compete.

Ethne's house, House Cawthorne, had turned out some of the most legendary warriors in the seven realms, which had made Ethne quite famous in the capital due to her sigil alone. But now she must lift her hood and hide her face. As the guards waved them inside, Lysa watched Ethne and knew that she was thinking the same thing: she would never again be welcomed to Adwean with laughter and cheers.

They didn't head immediately to the port. Instead, they decided to find another inn and get a meal and some much-needed rest first. They came to a tavern called the Dragon's Tooth and ate a hot meal at the bar. Everyone was very quiet, partly due to exhaustion and partly due to the anger between many of them. Liadan and Ava alone were talkative and mostly spoke to each other. Then they all went up to bed.

Saoirse, as ever, took first watch, standing at the window as everyone else rolled out their bedrolls on the floor and settled in near the hot hearth. Ava and Liadan took the bed – because Ava was pregnant and Liadan wanted to sleep next to her—and Ethne and Fionn joined them. Lysa watched bitterly from the hearth, thinking that it used to be her who shared the bed with Liadan, Ava, and Ethne. She felt almost as if Fionn had replaced her, and she knew now that she had no one to blame but herself: she had pushed Ethne away—away into the arms of Fionn!

"Are you not spent, fair Lysa?" Saoirse asked from the window.

Lysa was standing over the hearth, warming her hands. She could have used Liadan and Ava's bedroll – they had offered it – but she did not want to sleep. She didn't think she could. When she looked over, Saoirse was watching her sympathetically.

The old lion pulled a chair out from the nearby table and sat, knees spread. She gestured for Lysa to come to her, and holding down a blush, Lysa went to Saoirse and sat on her knee. Saoirse looked at Lysa with soft eyes, smoothing a hand down Lysa's hair.

"I'm tired of all the fighting," Lysa confessed. "I just want everything to be like it was before."

"Aye," agreed Saoirse. "I grow weary of it myself. And I admit, it was wrong of me to bed you whilst knowing how Ethne felt about you and without her permission."

Lysa made a tisking noise. "For the sake of the gods! I'm my own woman, Saoirse!"

Saoirse smiled. "Yes, you are. But the fact remains that lying with you, that disregarding Ethne's feelings, was wrong. But once I did it, it was like the damage was already done, and I couldn't help myself." She looked down at Lysa with hungry eyes, and Lysa's heart skipped a beat.

"You're so small and fiery," Saoirse whispered huskily. "It drives me wild."

Lysa trembled a little when Saoirse reached for the buckle on her leather chest guard. "Saoirse!" she protested, holding Saoirse at bay. "If Ethne sees, she might get angry!"

Saoirse ignored Lysa, continuing with the buckle and letting the leather chest guard fall with a soft jingle to the floor. Lysa looked anxiously at the bed, where Ethne lay sleeping on her back. Ethne was on the side close enough to hear them and see them. They were practically right in front of her.

"Look at me," Saoirse growled in a commanding voice that made Lysa's heart skip a beat, and she grabbed Lysa's face and turned her head – and kissed her passionately on the mouth. Lysa moaned against the kiss and felt her sex throbbing to life at once. As if she sensed Lysa's arousal, Saoirse's hand crammed down her pants and fingered her hard. Lysa gasped in delight.

"Your pussy is dripping," Saoirse whispered, her lips brushing Lysa's. She suddenly stood, setting Lysa on her feet – and bending her over the nearby table.

Lysa gasped as her cheek touched the cold wood. She could hear buckles jingling, then her trousers and panties were impatiently yanked down, and her eyes flew open wide as the sheepskin phallus of Saoirse's strap plunged fast and hard between the fat lips of her sex.

Lysa cried out in ecstasy as Saoirse moved against her, slamming the phallus in and out between her lips until they were dripping down her thighs. She was rocked so hard, her cheek was smashed against the table and was rising in her eye, blinding her. With her good eye, she could see Ethne on the bed, and her heart skipped a horrible beat in her chest: Ethne was awake and was quietly watching as Saoirse fucked her over the table!

Oh gods! Lysa thought wretchedly. Would Ethne get angry? Would she spring out of bed and attack Saoirse?

Whether or not Saoirse had noticed Ethne watching, Lysa couldn't tell. The old lion was wild in her lust, humping Lysa so hard that the table was shaking. She pushed Lysa's tunic up so that her hanging breasts were exposed and groped one as she continued to hump, slamming the phallus in, so that Lysa cried out shrilly and blushed to her hairline. She could feel her other breast swinging wildly and knew what it must've looked like to Ethne, her bent over, blushing and softly screaming, as Saoirse grunted and thrusted, as the thick leather phallus plunged fast between her pink lips, stroking her so deep and so *good.*

Why, oh, why was Ethne just lying there watching? The knight was lying on her back, head turned, staring at Lysa, and Fionn lay on Ethne's chest, sleeping peacefully. Then something else happened Lysa hadn't anticipated: Fionn's pale lashes fluttered open, and she went still, watching in paralyzed astonishment as Lysa was plowed over the table by Saoirse.

"By the gods," Saoirse grunted, "your pussy's so tight!" So saying, she kicked Lysa's legs wider apart, and the phallus plunged deeper, forcing a gasp of shocked delight from Lysa, whose eyes momentarily rolled back in a daze of pleasure. When she looked again, Ethne and Fionn were still watching her, and both of them were hungry-eyed and lusting.

"Your back is tight," panted Saoirse. "You must be coming—"

Lysa blushed a little: she was indeed climaxing. She was trying to hold it back and not let it happen before the staring eyes of Ethne and Fionn, but she couldn't contain her passion: her sex clenched on the phallus and a choked cry escaped her lips as she blushed and squirted helplessly down her own thighs.

Fionn was so fascinated by the sight of Lysa's climax that she had actually sat up on her elbows and watched with popping eyes. Ethne was also still watching and had sat up on her elbow, her nostrils flaring with desire.

"What are you waiting for?" said Saoirse, carefully pulling the phallus free (it squelched from the moisture of Lysa's sex, and she blushed in embarrassment). Saoirse stepped back. "Get over here, you two. You know you want to."

To Lysa's amazement, Ethne and Fionn rose from the bed. Ethne was in her underarmor and Fionn was in her skimpy linen under-robe. As Lysa continued bending over the table, panting to catch her breath, she saw them disappear behind her, and a moment later, felt their tongues lapping desperately at her sex.

Lysa gasped in shock as their tongues slapped her. She felt what was unmistakably Ethne's strong hand prying at her buttocks, pulling them apart to further expose her sex, and she blushed when a tongue slid in her sex, when another tongue slapped lovingly on her clitoris. Lysa shivered. Was this really happening? They were pleasuring her exquisitely. Who knew the little priestess had such a tongue on her?

And Fionn was shockingly ravenous for a woman of the cloth. She sucked on Lysa's clitoris until Lysa found herself panting desperately and trying to catch her breath, and even as Fionn was sucking her, she could feel Ethne's strong fingers plunging inside her. She tightened her sex on Ethne's fingers and heard Ethne's moan of approval. The knight fingered Lysa so gently, so deliciously, and Fionn was sucking so passionately on Lysa's clitoris that she squeezed her eyes shut and cried out, coming yet again. Her thighs trembled as she squirted down them yet another time, and she sank to the floor and caught herself with both hands.

Lysa bowed her head and panted. She blushed a little when Fionn kissed her cheek and whispered, "Won't you come to bed with us? I like the way you taste!"

"Fionn!" Lysa cried, shocked.

Ethne laughed.

"But it's true!" said Fionn, wide-eyed. She paused and admitted bashfully, "Yours is the first . . . I've never before . . . Though I've often dreamed . . ." She blushed to her hairline, and Lysa couldn't help thinking she was adorable.

Ethne took Lysa's hands and helped her to stand. Then she set about pulling up Lysa's panties and pants and buttoning her trousers shut for her. Fionn watched this, gazing at Lysa dotingly and sometimes fixing Lysa's mussed hair, and surrounded as she was by such affection from the pair of them, Lysa found it difficult to hate them anymore.

"Is all forgiven, sweet Lysa?" Ethne asked when she had finished adjusting Lysa's clothes for her.

Lysa gazed into Ethne's pretty, gray eyes and felt something in her relenting. "Yes," she breathed and couldn't hold back a smile. "Do you forgive me as well?"

"Well, I just ate your pussy something fierce," Ethne said, making Lysa blush, "so yes." So saying, she casually flipped Lysa over one shoulder, flipped Fionn over the other, and carried them both to the bed, where the three of them lay down and went to sleep, Lysa and Fionn each snuggled in Ethne's arms.

As Lysa drifted off to dreams, she thought that she *did* love Ethne. She truly did. But they wanted different things, just as she and Ava wanted different things, and because of that, one day, they would have to part ways.

But for right now? Lysa would love Ethne with all of her heart.

Map of Realm Illa

More From Ash Gray

Her First Knight
Book 6
The Flower of Adwean
Chapter 1

Ava didn't know what had happened to change things, but she was glad to see Lysa and Ethne getting along again. This in turn seemed to put Rowan and Saoirse in a cheerful mood, and once Rowan had stopped bickering with Ethne, the newlyweds continued doting on each other unperturbed.

Ava still couldn't believe she was married. She had never dreamt that she would be permitted to marry a woman, and such a beautiful, strong woman as Liadan.

And soon, they would have their first child. Ava's stomach was growing rounder everyday. She was starting to show through her traveling dress, and sometimes at night, she could feel the child moving as surely as she could feel the dragon moving in its egg. The child and the dragon would be born at the same time, she knew it, and they would grow together and become fast friends. Her head was filled with daydreams of her barbarian daughter riding the dragon against the clouds.

They left the Dragon's Tooth that morning after a hearty breakfast at the bar. Outside, it was another bright, sunny day, and Ava noticed the snow was beginning to melt. Spring was fast coming. She hoped camping on the road would be less dismal.

The party mounted their horses at the stables, and the crowds outside were so thick that they had to walk them at a slow pace. Ava sat the saddle before Liadan, for they shared the great chestnut Ava had purchased back in Hastow, and the princess watched wistfully as small children ran through the streets, giggling and shrieking and blowing soap bubbles.

Adwean, being such a huge city, was bustling with crowds. It was almost as crowded as the great capital where Ava had grown up. And it was bursting with color, for many noble houses were in Adwean and their banners waved everywhere from carriages, towers, and saddles.

The people of Adwean spoke excitedly of a late winter festival. It would happen that afternoon in the square. There would be drinking and dancing and games, and some of the knights would spar to win favors.

"Wintermas," said Ethne. She was riding the horse she shared with Fionn, and her hood was up to hide her face. Ava thought the Sparrow Knight's eyes were yearning and sad. Adwean was her home, after all, and had she not been banished, she would have been here, celebrating the holiday with her family.

"The Wintermas!" sighed Fionn with sad longing. "We always celebrate it at the temple. I suppose we shall miss it as we sail across the sea, but I think the gods shall understand our dire situation."

Rowan was riding at the head of the procession with Saoirse and smirked. "Have the gods forgiven you, then, for spreading your pretty thighs, dear Fionn?"

Fionn blushed brightly. "I – That is – the goddess Eyslath understands that I was seduced." She glanced up at Ethne with large, doting eyes.

Rowan chuckled. "Seduced, were you? So the fault lies with Ethne alone?"

"'Tis a burden I happily bear," said Ethne, and everyone laughed that time, even Lysa, who gazed at Ethne fondly.

Ava grinned long after the laughter had died down. She was glad to see everyone so merry. And why not? Their journey to Elloris needn't be a grim affair. Ava was going to have a child! They should be celebrating!

"Your home is beautiful, my knight," Fionn breathed, gazing around in such wonder that Ava knew she had never been to a big city before.

"My former home," said Ethne heavily, "for I am no longer permitted to set foot within. But yes, sweet Fionn, it is quite beautiful. My father is lord here, and the Lord Sparrow doth love to hold week-long festivals in honor of each holiday season. The festivities today shall last into the next week, I suspect."

"Your father is lord?" gasped Fionn in wonder.

"What? Ethne didn't tell you?" said Rowan, amused. "Back at the academy, she never shut up about it."

Ethne looked irritable that time, so Liadan interjected, explaining to Fionn with her serious, calm voice, "Our Knight of the Sparrow is a Cawthorne, my lady, one of the most famous houses in—"

Fionn gasped and twisted about, gazing up at Ethne. "You're a Cawthorne, my knight? One of you *thee* Cawthornes?"

Ethne smiled, looking very smug, and Ava held back a giggle when Lysa rolled her eyes.

"Yes, I used to spar at such festivals," answered Ethne. "It pleased my father – and several fine ladies."

Liadan chuckled, and Lysa rolled her eyes again.

"Yes, yes, you're a shameless dog," said Lysa, pulling her black mare up to walk it beside Ethne and Fionn. Her expression was weary but amused. "Everyone knows it but Fionn. She shall find out soon enough." Lysa looked away, leaving Fionn blinking and perplexed.

But somehow, Ava thought Lysa was wrong. Falling in love with Lysa had changed something in Ethne, and watching Ava and Liadan, Saoirse and Rowan all come into union had changed her still. The

Knight of the Sparrow wanted desperately what her friends had, and if she couldn't get it with Lysa, it was very obvious she was ready to settle with Fionn.

Perhaps, deep down, Lysa suspected it as well, for she suddenly rode a playful circle around their procession, as if to showoff her newly developed riding skills. And Ava had to admit that Lysa looked strong and beautiful, her thighs clenching the saddle, her hair rippling back, her breasts bouncing. She was doing it to tease Ethne, to prove herself more desirable than Fionn, and while Ethne was indeed watching Lysa's cantering with lust, Fionn was too. The little priestess watched Lysa ride with such burning hunger, it shocked Ava.

"Dost thou see something kiss-worthy?" Lysa teased Ethne as she cantered around their procession a second time.

"I shall do more than kiss you if I catch you!" Fionn said, making Ethne and Liadan laugh heartily.

Lysa was so startled by Fionn's words that she nearly careened in Saoirse. The Knight of the Lion calmly grabbed the reins of Lysa's horse, pulling it around to a stop as she told Lysa to stop prancing about.

"You shall draw attention to us," Saoirse grimly scolded, "and if you cease not, perhaps I shall let one of these guardsmen arrest you."

Lysa had never before been scolded by Saoirse, who she doted on girlishly, and Ava saw her cheeks flush with embarrassment and shame as she docilely fell into quietly riding beside the older woman. Saoirse seemed pleased by Lysa's obedience and gave the former handmaiden a kiss on the lips and a covert squeeze on her backside – which Saoirse had watched jiggling in the saddle when Lysa was riding a moment before.

Lysa looked flustered and pleased by the kissing and groping, but she was still embarrassed for having behaved like a child and didn't meet anyone's eye as they continued to ride.

"That Lysa is amazing," said Fionn, who was speaking in a low voice, so that only Ethne, Ava, and Liadan heard, for Ava and Liadan were riding nearby.

"She is beautiful and wild! I see why you love her," went on Fionn soothingly. "How you did weep in the chapel. Your poor heart!" Fionn reached back and sadly touched Ethne's face, her large blue eyes round with sympathy.

"Yes, well, it is now mended, thanks in great part to you, sweet Fionn," Ethne answered. "Pay it no more heed."

They rounded the corner and came to the square, where benches rose around a muddy dirt field. Colorful streamers, banners, and winter flowers were being hung, and people were already gathering in the stands.

"Is it noon already?" said Rowan in surprise.

"Indeed," answered Liadan, glancing at the high sun in the sky. "It is time for the sparring games."

"Oh!" Ava cried with longing when she saw a flock of giggling girls run by with winter flowers in their hair. They were pink-cheeked and pretty as they giggled shrilly about the handsome knights who would spar. She watched them hurry into the stands, where they sat together in their pretty gowns, still giggling. Their chaperone, an old woman in a simple servant's gown, took her time climbing up after them.

"Couldn't we stay and watch the sparring?" Ava moaned.

"Someone said there would be meat pie," said Rowan wistfully. "I haven't had meat pie in a full moon."

"And we could stay longer at the Dragon's Tooth," Liadan added. She leaned close and whispered in Ava's ear, "Extend our honeymoon."

Ava blushed and giggled.

"I could enter the sparring games," said Ethne dreamily, "for old time's sake."

"I could enter and make some coin," said Lysa, bright greediness in her eyes.

"You couldn't," Saoirse told her. "It's only for highborn."

"I could get a fake banner and pretend," Lysa insisted angrily. "You may hold sway over these knights, Saoirse, but I—"

Without warning, Saoirse caught Lysa's cheeks in her strong hand and kissed Lysa slowly on the lips. When the old lion had pulled away, Lysa looked a little dazed from the kiss and was blushing hotly.

"You will do as I command," Saoirse said quietly, "if you desire further affection from me."

Rowan laughed, watching on in great amusement.

Lysa humbly cast her lashes down, and Ava tried not to laugh as well: Lysa would do whatever she was told to keep getting Saoirse's skilled hands down her panties at night.

Saoirse held up her fist to stop the procession, and when the others had halted in the street, she guided her great tawny horse around to face them. Her serious eyes went from face to face in disbelief.

"Look how all of you sulk because you wish to linger here for the winter festival! As if we were on holiday!" Saoirse scolded. She nodded at Ava. "Princess, you carry the fate of your entire house there beneath your breasts, and you would jeopardize it to watch a sparring match?"

Ava wanted to fire back, but all she could do was sit there, overcome with shame and feeling like a silly child.

Saoirse looked to Ethne next. "And, Ethne. Before you fretted and moaned about setting foot here. Now you would put your life at risk for nostalgia?"

"It's all I have left!" Ethne snapped – with such venom that everyone looked around at her in wonder.

Ava's lips parted in surprise: Ethne's face was twisted with emotion and tears were in her eyes. They watched as she lifted small Fionn by her waist and set the little priestess on her feet in the mud.

Fionn's pale blue eyes panicked. "Ethne!" she cried, grabbing the horse's reins.

Ethne swallowed hard as tears coursed down her face, and her eyes when she gently pried Fionn's hands off were apologetic. Then she pulled her horse around and galloped off, forcing pedestrians to shriek and dive out of her path.

"Ethne!" Rowan yelled angrily, but Ethne kept galloping and didn't look back. "Gods dammit!" Rowan snarled.

Saoirse had already pulled her horse alongside Fionn, who was weeping into her hands. She leaned down and gently gathered little Fionn into the saddle with her.

Rowan looked at Saoirse. "What do we do?"

"We return to the inn," said Liadan, who was still gazing off after Ethne. Her blue eyes were concerned. She finally looked at Saoirse as she said, "Rowan and I shall pursue Ethne. You take the maidens back to the Dragon's Tooth."

Saoirse nodded, pulling her horse back around. "Be swift," she said. "We should have been on a ship for the eastern shore already."

Liadan nodded dutifully in return. She slid down from her horse and gently gathered Ava in her arms. Ava's lashes fluttered when – instead of being allowed to walk – she was carried like a precious package to Lysa's horse. Ava was touched by Liadan's coddling but also thought the knight was being a little neurotic.

Lysa blushed angrily, and Ava knew she was tired of being treated like one of the damsels. She wanted to go with Liadan and Rowan and said so through her teeth.

"You must take care of Ava for me," Liadan told her.

Lysa made a face. "Don't patronize me, Liadan! I want to help you find Ethne! She could be hurt!"

Liadan stood cradling Ava in her arms, looking annoyed and indecisive.

"Let the girl go with you," said Saoirse, who was watching Lysa fondly. "Rowan will return to the inn with me. I would rather she weren't caught up in your mess anyhow."

Liadan looked as if she wanted to argue with Lysa, but realizing that time was wasting, she grudgingly carried Ava to Rowan's horse instead. Ava settled in the saddle before Rowan, and her heart fluttered when Liadan took her hand and kissed it.

"Return to me quickly," Ava begged.

"I shall, my wife, if fate allows it," answered Liadan. Her eyes softened and she touched Ava's face. Then she turned, mounted her horse, and galloped after Ethne with Lysa at her side.

Don't miss out!

Visit the website below and you can sign up to receive emails whenever Ash Gray publishes a new book. There's no charge and no obligation.

https://books2read.com/r/B-A-ZRKF-PWEBC

BOOKS 2 READ

Connecting independent readers to independent writers.

Also by Ash Gray

A Time of Darkness
Time's Arrow
The Infinite Athenaeum

Clan of the Cave Bear
Taken by the Chieftess
Passed Around
Keeping Warm
Her Pretty Pet
Dominated
Seduced
Caught
Savaged

Cyber Mech
Good With Her Hands

Fallen Stars

Fragile Hearts
Broken Minds
Digital Heartbeats
Electric Souls
Metal Bones

Her First Knight
The Knight of the Wild
Sparrow Song
Rowan's Hammer
The Dragon of Almara
Sanctuary
The Flower of Adwean
The Halls of Erinyel
The Daughter of Light
The Tomb of Azmon
Queen Liadan

Knight of Fire
The Queen of Swords
The Three of Goblets
The Queen of Wands
The Queen of Goblets
The Star
The World

Knights of Passion
The Queen's Lust

Handfasting the Warrior Queen
The Revenge of Raven's Cross
The Light of Lythara
Taming the Wolf Knight
The Mermaids of Menosea
The Fairy Queen of Elwenhal
The Dragon of Edhen
Essential Selene
Hearth and Home
Aereth's Return
The Fairy Ring
The Main Course
Knights of Passion: The Complete Series

Knights of Vallor
Saving Salia
Raven Spirit
Eryet's Fountain
The Daughter of Idet
The Mirror of Iovar
Aine's Athenaeum
Bone and Fire
Princess Eydis

Ona of Ozmora
The Amulet of Tizra
The Bandit Queen of Crystal Falls
The Council of Eldor
The Sword of Avara
Wicked Things in the Wilds

Pirates of Artusa
Stolen Booty
Taking Her Sword
Marooned

Tales of the Blood Moon Coven
Bloodlust
The Hidden Memory
Whispered Names
Morbid Fascination
Bending to Her Will
Blood Rage
Prey
Hunted
Voyeuristic Intentions
Interludes and Ecstasy

The Assassin's Kiss
Crossed Daggers
Swordplay

The Chronicles of Omicron
The Thieves of Nottica
The Watchtower of Rustoria

The Dragon Riders of Valheera
Birthday Surprises

The Dreamscape
Out of Mind
Recalling Color

The Last Queen of Qorlec
Project Mothership
The Harvest
The Suns of Anarchy
The Light-year Lion
Moon Fire
Exiled Stars
Zora's Stone

The Legend of Kiva
The Starlight Stair

The Pussycat Chronicles
The Heist
Broken Hearts and Brain Damage
Candy, Sweat, and Regret
Lip Gloss and Loose Women

Witch Xim
Rezzora's Workshop

Standalone
Qorth
Fall Apart World
Unicorn Blood

About the Author

Ash Gray is a lesbian living in California. She writes lesfic (aka fiction for lesbians) in science fiction, fantasy, and paranormal settings.